NAUGHTY:

Two's Enough, Three's a Crowd

NAUGHTY:

Two's Enough, Three's a Crowd

BRENDA HAMPTON

URBAN
Renaissance
www.urbanbooks.net

Urban Books, LLC
78 East Industry Court
Deer Park, NY 11729

ISBN 13: 978-1-60162-207-5
ISBN 10: 1-60162-207-4

First Trade Printing February 2009
First Mass Market Printing March 2010
Printed in the United States of America

10 9 8 7 6 5 4 3 2 1

Distributed by Kensington Publishing Corp.
Submit Wholesale Orders to:
Kensington Publishing Corp.
C/O Penguin Group (USA) Inc.
Attention: Order Processing
405 Murray Hill Parkway
East Rutherford, NJ 07073-2316
Phone: 1-800-526-0275
Fax: 1-800-227-9604

ACKNOWLEDGMENTS

Always, a special thanks to my family, readers, book clubs, bookstores, and friends. To Carl and Martha Weber, and the Urban Books family, your dedication to my literary career is truly a blessing. I can't think of any other team of people in this industry who I enjoy working with more. I owe all of you a heartfelt thanks.

An extended thanks to my Heavenly Father for not being with me only when times are great, but for looking over me when times are hard. I give all praises to You and look forward to the future that You have waiting for me . . . whatever it may be.

NAUGHTY:

Two's Enough, Three's a Crowd

JAYLIN

Eeny, Meeny, Miney and Moe. I got Eeny and Meeny, now all I need is Miney and Moe. I love women; they're what make the world go round. So, the more of them I have, the better off I am. Settling down for me is out of the question. There's enough of me to share with as many women as I want—as long as they meet my standards. And standards, high standards, I do have. Any woman who wants to be considered must be not only bodacious, but she must have a degree, be able to cook, have job stability, drive a nice car, be African American, have no kids, and most importantly, she must be willing to cater to my every need. If not, then she ain't worth my time.

I'm dealing with two sistas right now who meet most of the above, but they're starting to slack on me.

Slacking causes me to get bored, and when I'm bored, major changes have to take place.

Nokea is the kind of woman you can definitely take home to Mama, but since Mama ain't around anymore, there's no need for that. Nokea is a pretty, petite thing with curves in all the right places, and her skin is so smooth that sometimes I'm forced to call her Silk. She's got beautiful, big round eyes that go well with her luscious, soft lips. Her hair is shiny, black, and barely long enough for me to run my fingers through. But my true attraction to Nokea is her loyalty to me and her independence. She's a smart woman, and she ain't trying to reach into my bank account for nothing. Most of all, she got my back—and I have hers. She's my rock. I care about her more than any woman I've ever dated.

The problem I have with Nokea is she ain't upping no booty. She firmly believes a woman shouldn't give herself to a man unless she's married to him. And even though I respect her needs, I got needs too. Fucking needs. At least a minimum of three times a week. I expressed my concerns to Nokea, but she insists on depriving me. I don't play games, so I have never lied to her about my desires for other women. I guess she accepts it because other than that, I'm quite a catch. When she needs me, I've been there. When she's lonely, I hold her. When she calls, I'm there to talk. Since we've been together, I've only improved her life. I've shown her the qualities of a real man. A lack of sex is the only problem between us.

That's where Felicia comes in. Felicia's bad. She gives it to a brotha when, where, and however he wants it. Lay it smack dead on the table and pow-dow, brotha be all up in it! She's got a smooth, soft, and juicy dark-brown ass and nice firm breasts to match.

Her long braids go well with her round chocolate face. And her smile, it's to die for. All she gotta do is lay one on me and I melt.

She works as an architect and makes pretty good money. Of course, her salary is nowhere near mine, but what the hell . . . there's not too many people kicking it down like me. The biggest problem with Felicia is she's fucking cheap. She never spends money on me, and if she does, it has to be a special occasion like my birthday or something—or if I've fucked her brains out and she wants to be generous.

As for Nokea, she buys me everything. Sends me encouraging cards when I'm feeling down. Takes me to dinner and pays. Even buys me clothes when she sees something I might like.

I just can't decide which one of them accents me better. That's why I don't choose one woman over the other. One woman can't give me everything I want, and for that matter, no two. So, now I'm on the prowl again. Looking for somebody to help fill this emptiness I've been feeling lately. Looking for somebody I can add to my collection.

More realistically, I need some more pussy. Getting sort of tired of the same stuff, and since my baby's mama, Simone, jetted with my child, I can't run to her anymore for a li'l something on the side. Things were just all right with us, but when she told me she was pregnant, I had to man-up and take care of my responsibilities.

I enjoyed spending time with my baby girl, Jasmine, and she brought so much happiness to my life. Then, one day, when Jasmine was almost one year old, Simone did the unthinkable and left. She had a boyfriend in the army, and according to the brief letter that I received in the mail, they were going to get married. The letter implied that her husband would now take my place, and Jasmine would be told that he was her father.

I could've killed Simone. When I jetted to her house to see what was up, it was vacant. I was so hurt, and as the weeks, months, and years have gone by, I feel as if a huge part of me is missing. Damn Simone for making me feel this way. This is another reason why I have a difficult time falling in love with women. No doubt, they can do some stupid shit!

In the meantime, Felicia be setting that pussy out for me, but I know she can do better. I've been trying to ease myself into Nokea too, but she ain't having it. So, a brotha gotta do what he gotta do to make sure his needs are being met. If I ain't happy, nobody's happy. And one thing Mama always taught me is to make myself happy before I make anybody else happy.

I miss Mama. A mugger robbed and killed her as she walked home from work one night. I was only nine years old and had to live in an orphanage until my Aunt Betty came to get me damn near two years later. Living with her was hell. She was a dope addict and treated her kids and me like shit. I moved out at six-teen, but kept my butt in school. Living on the streets wasn't no joke, so I quickly got a job at a restaurant. My charming personality brought in good tips, and that helped pay for my one-room apartment.

When I turned eighteen, my grandfather died and left me part of his estate. I didn't understand why because we never had a good relationship. Hell, I barely knew the man, but when my Aunt Betty told me about the money, I was ecstatic. I used some of the money to further my education, invested a large sum of it in the stock market, and outright purchased a million-dollar home in Chesterfield, Missouri. Now, I'm the number one stock broker at Schmidt's Brokerage Firm, and I rarely look back at my horrific past.

A few months ago, I got a call from Aunt Betty begging for money. She claimed she had kicked her habit and needed a new start, but I ain't no fool. The money I work hard for ain't never gonna be used for smoking no crack. I told her I was on my way to give it to her, but never showed. I hope she got the picture.

Unlike my rough relationship with her, I do have a close connection with my cousin, Stephon. He's like a brother to me. He turned out pretty cool after being raised by my Aunt Betty. Got his own barbershop and makes decent money. He's the only person I consider as family, and the rest of them can go to hell, especially my father.

Before Mama was killed, my father and I had a pretty cool relationship. They weren't married, but he'd always come to the house to see me or take me with him. Aunt Betty said that Mama's sudden death took a toll on him, but did he have to run off and leave me behind? Who knows where he is now. The last time I saw him was at Mama's funeral. I was sure we'd leave together, but when I looked around, he was nowhere to be found. He left me without anyone in my life to love, and that was something I would never be able to forgive.

Now, I'm doing things my way. I'm very particular about who I let be a part of my life, and I only keep positive people in my company. If I feel some bullshit about to go down, I jet. Ain't got time for it. My main focus is my career, my money, my body—I work out every single day—and the gorgeous ladies in my life. Those things add to my confidence and allow others to view me as a well put together black man.

NOKEA

I've known Jaylin Jerome Rogers since we were kids, and during our elementary years, we became the best of friends. His mama worked with mine at a cookie factory in South St. Louis, and they too were good friends. Jaylin finally noticed me at twenty-one, and now at the age of twenty-nine, our relationship is going strong. He's a year older than me, and he has everything I want my man to have. Whenever he isn't too busy, he finds time to make me smile, to make me laugh, and to just plain old comfort me. I can ask him for just about anything, and without hesitation he delivers. Eventually, I think he's going to settle down, and when he does, I'll be waiting. I have a special bond with him—more than any other woman he's been with. And he told me that when the time comes, I would be The One.

So, my future is already in the making. Jaylin has a good job as an investment broker and makes about $500,000 a year. That doesn't even include the money he inherited from his grandfather's estate. The only reason that he works is to keep himself busy. He needs a beautiful, educated woman like me in his life, and if he thinks he can make it without me, he's crazy. I was there when his mama died and when his baby's mama, Simone, took off with his daughter. He cried on my shoulder. I promised to always be there for him, even when we were kids. To this day, I've never let him down, and I'm not going anywhere.

I'm well aware of his relationship with Felicia, but she doesn't have what it takes to keep him. I, on the other hand, do. She doesn't realize that a piece of booty isn't all Jaylin's looking for. He needs so much more than that, and since I've had years to observe him, I know what he needs versus what he wants. In the end, I'll be the one to give it to him. She's only temporary, and I'll still be there once she's gone, just like all the others.

See, while Jaylin makes it clear that he doesn't want a commitment, I make it clear that I'm saving myself for my husband. We've come close many times, but he knows I stand my ground. He respects me for not giving my body to anyone but my future husband. He also knows Daddy taught me well and I wouldn't do anything to dishonor his wishes. I know Jaylin has needs; that's why I try not to let his other relationships upset me. Besides, even though there have been plenty of women in Jaylin's life, after a while, they become history while I'm still around. Why? Because I'm connected with the most important thing on him. And that, of course, is his heart. No woman will be woman enough to take that from me. Deep down, even he knows it.

As kids, our parents said we were destined to be together, and there's no way he's going to forget what his mama told him. So, some day, hopefully soon, I'll be Mrs. Nokea Rogers and having the time of my life!

FELICIA

The first time I saw Jaylin, I knew he was the one for me. He stepped out of his black SL 500 Roadster convertible Mercedes Benz at Tony's Restaurant on Market Street and asked for my digits. Even though he was entertaining someone else that night, I didn't care and neither did he. His dark Armani suit and his curly black hair were what instantly attracted me to him. I could smell the money on him, and I thanked God for sending him my way. When Jaylin removed his tinted round glasses, I got a glimpse of his light-gray bedroom eyes and was hooked! I ain't never been excited about no light-skinned, tall brotha, but Jaylin had it going on.

After one day of talking, we were rolling in the sack. I held his broad shoulders and damn near broke my back trying to make sure this brotha called me the next day. I was successful, and he's been calling me ever since— mostly late nights, after he's exhausted from all the ups and downs of the stock market, which, by the way, can be a pain. His mood swings aren't anything to play with, but every time he starts to trip, I get up and go.

I know Jaylin loves me, but he has a funny way of showing it. This homely bitch, Nokea, thinks he's so deeply in love with her that he can't even see straight. But, I continue to deliver breaking news to her: Jaylin couldn't care less about a woman trying to cater to him like his mama. He tells me often that I'm the true happiness in his life.

When we come together as one, our salaries combined will speak volumes. Ain't a damn thing we'll want for. We've already been to Jamaica, to Paris, and even to Hawaii together. I paid my own way, but that's because I can handle my own, and . . . Jaylin can sometimes be cheap. Considering all of the money he has, I don't quite understand why he doesn't splurge on me. He spends just enough on me to get by, and that's only because he knows in order to get something, you've got to give something. He's lucky that I don't trip off the money thing too much. Only when he starts to slack on the "D" thing will I consider it.

Still, as far as I know, he hasn't even taken a vacation with Nokea. What man wants to be on vacation with a woman he can't touch? I'm the one who holds the key to his heart, and if he chooses her over me, he'd be a fool. She ain't even giving him no twang. Now, what kind of woman plays that crap in this day and age? How can she be foolish enough to even step to a brotha like Jaylin Rogers and play that "I'm saving myself" bullshit? All she's doing is saving up for a big disappointment, because I'm working him with everything I have. I'm the only pussy he's laying into right now, and hopefully that'll be forever.

He stressed that as long as I continue to give him what he wants, he'll make sure I play a valuable part in his life. So valuable, that one day, hopefully soon, I'll be Mrs. Jaylin Jerome Rogers, and feeling on top of the world!

1

FELICIA

Dinner was spectacular. Jaylin didn't seem to be his usual self, but since work always seemed to occupy his mind, I didn't push. No matter how tired he was, he almost always found time to make us dinner on Friday nights. I had offered to help tonight, but he wanted credit for the well seasoned porterhouse steaks and garlic potatoes.

I cleaned off the table and piled the dishes in the sink so I could wash them later. Jaylin went into his room to lie down because he insisted his head was banging. I peeked into his room to check on him, but instead of resting, he was on the phone. I knew he was probably talking to that bitch, Nokea. He always acted like she was his mama or something, and every time something tragic happened, he leaned on her shoulder. It bothered me a bit, but I wasn't no fucking psychiatrist. I didn't have time to listen to his drama. My job was to satisfy his physical needs, and that's what I intended to do.

I went back into the kitchen and started on the dishes. Jaylin had a dishwasher, but he was a particular brotha. Real tidy. Neat as a pin. According to him, a dishwasher didn't do the job he wanted it to do. He had to scrub the dishes himself to make sure they were sparkling clean. Why buy a fucking dishwasher if you ain't gonna use it? Didn't make sense to me. He said he bought it just to blend in with the other stainless steel appliances in his kitchen.

He wasted a lot of money, and rarely used many of the items in his house, like the silver pots that dangled above the black marble-topped island in the middle of the kitchen floor. Never been cooked in at all. When he made dinner for us, he had another set he used. The hanging set was just for show, just like the furniture that he traveled the world to find. We'd never eaten at his dinette set, and if you'd dare take a seat in one of the soft white leather chairs, he'd have a fit.

We ate in his bonus room, designed specifically for his guests. It had a theatre-sized TV, a pool table, and a cocktail bar with every kind of alcohol you can think of. There was also a mustard-colored leather sofa that surrounded the room. We used it for fucking when we couldn't make it to his bedroom.

I dried the last plate and laid it neatly on the shelf. Soft music played on the intercom throughout the house, and I heard Jaylin open the kitchen door. When I turned, he stood naked, staring at me with lust in his eyes. The sight of his muscular body always weakened me, so I laid the towel on the counter to see what was on his mind.

"Jaylin, baby, are you okay?"

"I'm fine. I just came down to see what was taking you so long. My dick doesn't stay hard all night, you know."

With his hands, he tossed his dick from side to side and I watched it grow. No doubt, it looked delicious.

"I was just finishing up. Besides, I didn't think you were ready yet. The last time I checked, you were still on the phone."

"Well, I'm off now, so when you get finished in here, I got something waiting for you up there," he said, pointing in the direction of his bedroom.

"I'll be up in a minute. Keep my spot warm for just a few more minutes."

Jaylin grinned and left the kitchen. I took a look at his tight, muscular ass and started to rush myself. Then I realized that if he came down later and saw something out of place, he'd throw a fit. I wasn't in no mood to hear his mouth, so decided to take my time.

When I was finished, I slid out of my sexy red dress in the kitchen and dropped it on the floor. Then I left my black bra on the banister at the bottom of the staircase, and tied my black lace panties around the rail when I reached the top of the stairs. I removed my hair clip and let my braids fall down my back. I followed Jaylin's scent to his room and opened the double tinted-glass doors.

Jaylin lay there asleep. He looked so handsome and peaceful I didn't want to wake him. My pussy had other plans, so I eased onto his California king-sized bed and lay next to him. I rubbed my fingers across his thick eyebrows to straighten them and kissed his cheek.

He slowly opened his eyes. "What took you so long?" he mumbled.

"I came right up, but you had already fallen asleep." By the time I finished speaking, his eyelids were already fading.

Friday nights were becoming a disappointment. Jaylin and I didn't used to miss a beat when it came to sex, but for the last three weeks, he'd been tripping. He used to wake up just to lay it on me; it wasn't like him to be too tired for sex. Something was wrong, but I couldn't put my finger on it. I fell asleep thinking about what was troubling him, only to wake up later to the sound of his loud voice.

"Felicia!" I heard him yell from downstairs. "Felicia! Why is your dress in the middle of my damn kitchen floor? And your bra and panties have no place being where they are. You of all people know I don't like that shit!" He stomped up the steps with my dress tightened in his hand.

"Damn, I'm sorry. But you ain't gotta get all upset about it at three o'clock in the morning," I said, standing naked at the top of the stairs. "It wouldn't have stayed there all day because you know I gotta wear something home, don't I? So what's the big fuss?"

Jaylin didn't say a word. He tossed my dress to me and cut his eyes, as if he wanted to tear me apart.

I wrapped my dress around my naked body and went back into his bedroom. I saw him bent over, while turning on the water in his Jacuzzi tub. I stood in the doorway and watched. Hot steam filled the bathroom, and after he stepped in the tub, he laid his head back on a contoured pillow.

"So," I said, removing my dress from around me. "Would you like some company in there?"

"No, not right now." He closed his eyes and appeared to be in deep thought.

"And, why not?" I asked with a slight attitude.

"Because, right now, I want to be alone. Before your mouth gets going, Felicia, I ain't up for a bunch of questions. So, either go to bed, or leave. Preferably, the door awaits you."

"Jaylin, look, I'm confused. What did I do to upset you tonight? I know the stock market is down but I don't want to be dumped on because you're losing your money."

He ignored me, got out of the tub, poured himself a glass of Moët, and got right back in. I know he told me to leave, but I had no plans to do so. I got right back in bed and turned on the flat-screen TV on the wall in front of me.

I started to nod off, but then I heard Jaylin on the phone again. This time, it sounded like it was one of his boys, because I heard him say, "Man, she be tripping." Since he was full of laughs and seemed to pick up a new attitude, I figured it had to be Stephon on the phone.

Stephon was cool. He wasn't as devious or arrogant as Jaylin, but they did have a lot in common. They looked like brothers; other than Stephon being bald and dark chocolate, they still resembled each other in many ways. When it came to their bodies, I couldn't tell which one was in better shape. Jaylin even treated Stephon like a brother. Bought him a barbershop in the Central West End, gave him half on the white 500-series BMW he drove, and recently gave him five grand to take this bitch he'd only known for two weeks on a cruise.

When I first saw Stephon, I considered getting with him, but by then, Jaylin had me hooked. Even Stephon's sexy hazel eyes couldn't sway me. But now that Jaylin was being difficult, maybe I should think twice.

Jaylin had the nerve to always call me cheap, but every time we went out lately, he was talking that "split the bill" crap. We could go through the drive-thru at McDonald's and he'd be having his hand out, asking for half.

It didn't used to be like that. I guess in the beginning, he did what he had to do to keep me; but now, if it wasn't for the good loving he was putting down, I would've been gone. I'd had plenty of brothas, but nobody set me out like he did, especially if the stock market was booming and he was making money. Brotha be working this ass all night long . . . sucking me dry. And then, we'd wind the night down with a bottle of chardonnay. That's the Jaylin I fell in love with. He'd better come out of this shell soon. If not, I would be looking for another brotha to give it to me like he used to. It would be tough, but sista gotta do what a sista gotta do!

I could hear the water running down the drain and watched Jaylin as he dried off. When he came into the bedroom, I pretended to be asleep. From the bottom of the bed, he lifted the satin sheets and crawled between my legs. I felt his thick lips kiss my thighs, and I trembled as his tongue lightly touched them. I interrupted him and lifted his head from between my legs.

"I thought you were anxious for me to leave."

He let out a deep sigh. "Felicia, why don't you just

go? You've messed up my mood twice tonight, and my dick ain't even excited anymore." He moved next to me in bed.

"Would you like to talk about what's troubling you? Your attitude really stinks."

"I told you once I ain't got time to talk. If you want to talk, call up one of your girlfriends. They'll listen to you. All I was trying to do is get my fuck on. And since I can't do that, see ya." He turned his back to me and pulled the sheets over his head.

I'd had enough of Jaylin for one night, and put my dress back on. I grabbed my bra from the bottom handrail and jetted. I left my panties on the top stair for memories. Wasn't no telling when I was coming back. I'd have to try him another day, a day when he wasn't clowning like he was tonight. Knowing him, that day would probably be tomorrow.

2

JAYLIN

Felicia knew she be bullshitting. If I could have just gotten that woman to pick up after herself, she'd be all right with me. At five in the morning, she left me horny as hell with a dick that needed some direction. It was times like this that I hated being intimate with only one woman, and that shit had to change.

Instead of being alone, I called Nokea to come over and keep me company. She was an early bird and didn't mind coming over to see me. Before she got there, I slid in a porn movie and went to work on myself. Didn't make no sense for a man like me to have to get off like that, but a brotha gotta do what he gotta do to keep himself happy.

The doorbell rang and I ran downstairs to get it. My

baby was nice enough to come all the way over here to keep me company. She knew how much I hated being alone and would always come when I needed her to. I opened the door, and the smell of Nokea's sweet perfume hit me.

"Thanks for coming, baby," I said, giving her a tight hug.

"You sounded like something was wrong. Are you okay?"

"I'm cool. I had an awkward dream and couldn't get back to sleep."

"Well, I'm here. Do you want me to make you a drink or something?" she asked, walking upstairs to my bedroom. My mind left me for a minute as I visualized myself pounding the perfect little ass in front of me.

"I already had a drink before you came."

"That's not all you had before I came," she said, picking up Felicia's panties from the top handrail. "Who's been over here, Jaylin?"

"Baby, you know I ain't gonna lie to you; Felicia left not too long ago. She got upset with me because I didn't feel like having sex. Don't be upset. It ain't nothing but a fuck thang," I explained.

"Must you keep that trifling woman in your life? You act like you can't go without sex. If I can go without, I know you can. I'm just not sure how much more of this I can take."

"Don't go giving up on us, all right? I got needs, baby, and it's not that easy for me to go without sex. Since you're saving yourself, I have to make other arrangements. I know it's not what you want to hear, but it's the truth."

Nokea walked into my bedroom and pulled my Gucci sheets off the bed.

"Get me some clean sheets, Jaylin. I'm not going to lay my body on some sheets I know for a fact she laid on tonight."

Without a fuss, I went to the linen closet and got some clean sheets so I didn't have to hear Nokea's mouth for the rest of the night. She lay next to me and didn't say anything else about Felicia. As a matter of fact, she ended up falling asleep in my arms. I held her instead of her holding me, but I didn't mind. I knew what I put her through was wrong, but I needed more than just Nokea.

The next day, I found what I was looking for. I was going through my normal Saturday-morning workout, lifting weights at the gym, and she walked in. She asked if I was using a towel that was neatly folded on the rail beside me.

"No," I said, checking out her smooth, sweaty breasts as I handed the towel to her. "This towel is for anyone who needs to use it."

"Then, I guess that's me. I'm so exhausted from my new aerobics class and I don't think I'm going to be able to keep up." She wiped the dripping sweat from her curvaceous body and my eyes stayed glued to her. "So, what's your name?" she asked.

"It's, Jaylin . . . Jaylin Rogers. And yours?"

"Scorpio Valentino."

"Scorpio who? That's an unusual name."

"Valentino. My mother is black and my father is Italian."

"Oh, I see," I said while looking her over. She wasn't the type of woman I normally dated, but I couldn't deny my immediate attraction to her. Her eyes searched me over too. I'd seen that kind of look many, many times before. She wanted me between her legs, and I wasn't about to walk away from this one. I interrupted while she was speaking.

"Say, uh, I need to get back to my workout. Would it be too much trouble if I asked for your number?"

"I guess not, but I prefer that you give me your number. I'll call you."

I watched her wipe around her belly ring right above the good stuff. She didn't have a pen, so I whispered my number in her ear. She repeated the number to me and promised to call.

As she walked away, I watched her long, bouncing, curly hair move from side to side and her ass jiggle like it was calling my name. Now, that there was my kind of woman. She could definitely become number three in my life. And since she couldn't keep her eyes off my chest and the big bulge in my pants, it was obvious she liked what she saw too.

I was thinking about having sex with Scorpio, until Stephon came out of nowhere and smacked the back of my neck.

"Man, that shit hurt," I yelled.

"Fool, I saw you checking out that fine-ass woman with that bodacious body. I tried to grab her myself, but when I saw her step to you, I backed off. While you were lifting weights, I saw her staring at your ass like she wanted to come eat you alive."

"She was pretty nice looking, wasn't she? I gave her my digits. I hope she calls me tonight. I'd love to add those panties to my collection. If not, I'm gonna call and apologize to Felicia for last night and see if she'll come shake a brotha down."

"You know damn well she'll come. That pussy got your name written all over it. She hooked, and I mean bad. Shit, sometimes I wish I had it like that. These knuckleheads I be going out with just be looking for a damn handout. When a motherfucker gonna start handing me some shit? That's what I wanna know."

"What happened to that chick you took on that cruise? I thought everything was cool with y'all."

"Please. I got those panties on the cruise and that was it. When we came back, I had to let that ass go. Wasn't worth your money or my time. Besides, she was married. Her husband came to my shop and tried to punk me. I had to call the police to get his crazy ass out of there. Wasn't my fault he wasn't sticking it to her like I was."

"Damn, dog, that's messed up. You be careful messing with those scandalous-ass women. What you need to do is step up to my zone—start requiring qualifications and setting rules when it comes to your women. Don't just give your dick or your trust to anybody."

"I thought one of your rules was to only date black women. That cutie who stepped out of here just a minute ago wasn't black. She looked like she was mixed with something—if not damn near white."

"Yeah, I know. But there has to be an exception when it comes to a woman that fine."

"I hear you, my brotha, but don't go breaking all the rules unless you wanna wind up like me—with crazy women who seek a provider."

"Naw, dog. Never."

Stephon headed to the barbershop and I headed to

Victoria's Secret at the Galleria to find Felicia something nice to make up for last night. I also picked up a dozen red roses at Schnucks in Ladue just to make her feel extra special. It wasn't often that I did nice things for Felicia, but after seeing Scorpio, I felt kinda horny, and Felicia was my only option. I figured I had some making up to do before she'd give me any.

Her gray GS 300 Lexus was in the driveway, so I knew she was home. I rang the doorbell and leaned against the screen door. I held the roses behind my back with one hand and held the bag from Victoria's Secret up with my finger so she could see it.

She opened the door and her eyes widened, especially when she saw what I had for her. She was all over me.

"Damn, woman, don't get too close. I'm still sweaty from my workout."

"I can't help it, baby. Is this for me?" she asked, taking the Victoria's Secret bag from my hand.

"Yes. I want you to go put this on for me. Now!"

She pulled the pink tissue paper from the bag and looked inside. Then she turned it upside down and shook it. There was nothing inside, as I'd changed my mind about giving her the negligee and saved it for another time.

"Jaylin, there's nothing inside of this bag," she said, standing with her hands on her hips.

"I know. That's what I want you to go put on for me: nothing."

"Cute. Really cute."

Felicia took the roses from my hand and went into the kitchen to put them in a vase she already had from my previous flowers. I stood and watched, as I thought about my plans with Nokea tonight. I told her we'd have dinner, but there might be a slight delay.

"I just wanted to tell you I'm sorry for the way I behaved last night. I'm losing money every day in the stock market and I don't like that. I don't mean to shut you out, but the less I talk about it, the better," I said.

"Jaylin, I understand." She wrapped her arms around my neck. "That's why I don't bother you about anything. I don't want my man stressing all the time, because you ain't no good to me if you're stressed."

"Well, I ain't stressing now." I rubbed my hands on her fat, juicy chocolate ass.

"And I ain't stressing either, so you know what that means."

"It means I gotta jump in the shower so I can get myself ready for some of your sweetness."

"Well, you know where to go, and after you finish, this here will be waiting for you over there," she said, taking off her clothes and pointing to her room down the hall.

I smiled and watched her prance her sexy ass to the bedroom. I had to be out of my mind tripping with a woman like Felicia. Sista couldn't give more than what she was already giving. But I still needed more than just Felicia. I couldn't stop thinking about that sweet little piece of ass I saw today, but was forced to focus on Felicia right now.

I hopped in the shower, and then made my way to the bedroom so Felicia could help me release the tension I'd been feeling lately. No problem there. She rode me like a jockey trying to win a race, and then placed those soft little lips on my goodness to finish the job. The feeling always had me on cloud nine, but after today, I wondered if our relationship would survive another woman joining my circle.

3

NOKEA

I waited patiently for Jaylin to come home, but it neared six o'clock in the evening and he was a no show. I hoped he hadn't forgotten about our plans tonight. Every Saturday, we'd go catch a movie or go to dinner. Sometimes we'd go see a play, depending on what was at the Fox Theater. It wasn't like him not to call me all day, but since I had a key to his place, I decided I'd go to his house and wait for him.

After sitting at his place for another hour and watching Wheel of Fortune, I decided to rummage through his belongings. I always did that when I was alone at his house. It was the only way I could keep up with what was really going on with him. Now, if I asked, he'd tell me; but I had to pretend like I didn't care.

I'd already seen some naked pictures of Felicia and

some of his ex-girlfriends in a shoebox at the top of his closet and they disgusted me. I didn't understand how women could stoop so low by flaunting around naked pictures of themselves. Wasn't no telling what Jaylin did with these pictures. I knew his boys had probably seen them, and there was no way I was going to let his friends know what my goods looked like. Hell, Jaylin barely knew. Well, he knew what it looked like, but he didn't know what it felt like.

I was checking out this one disgusting picture of this chick with her leg resting on her shoulder when I heard the front door shut. I quickly threw the picture in the box and shoved it in the closet where it belonged. Jaylin jogged up the steps and I walked out of his bedroom to greet him.

"Hey, baby," he said, opening his arms to hug me. I didn't bother to hug him back, and instead stood with my arms by my sides.

Jaylin noticed my demeanor and gave me a quick peck on my cheek. "I saw your car in the driveway. How long have you been here?"

I folded my arms and followed him into the bedroom. "Uh . . . maybe just a few hours waiting on you to come home. Why didn't you call? And why are you so late?"

"I got caught up at the gym earlier, and then I went to apologize to Felicia for last night."

"Apologize for what? You said she was the one who left you."

"She did, but I wanted to apologize for my bad attitude, that's all. I don't like anybody leaving my house upset with me about my mood swings."

"And I'm sure you made it up to her. Just in case

you didn't notice, it's Saturday. According to you, this is our day. So, what are you doing spending time with Felicia? You could've called and apologized to her over the phone."

"Nokea, what's been up with you lately? You know this ain't nothing new. I don't like nobody upset with me, and I'm always willing to apologize when I'm wrong. So, without the hassle, let me get out of these clothes and take a shower so we can go," he said, taking off his sweaty, pussy-smelling clothes.

I turned my back, seething with anger as I went downstairs on the couch until he got ready. It was times like this when a huge part of me wanted to walk away from this relationship and never look back. Knowing that Jaylin had been with Felicia today was painful, and as I visualized the two of them in my mind, I wanted to get off the couch and run as fast as I could. I kept telling myself that I had a choice, but my decision had always been to hang in there.

Jaylin hurried down the steps wearing an off-white silk shirt and black wide-legged pants that fit him nicely around the waist. His shirt had a few buttons undone so I could get a glimpse of his muscular chest. He'd trimmed his beard and goatee so thin that I could barely see them, and his gray eyes shone as he walked into the living room and asked if I was ready to go.

"Yes, I'm ready. Been ready for quite a while now," I griped.

"So, what's the plan for tonight? If you don't know, I got a place in mind."

"Oh yeah, and where might that be?"

"There's a restaurant, The Hampshire, where we can sit on the terrace overlooking downtown St. Louis.

The scenery is off the chain, and I want to share an enjoyable dinner with my number one lady this evening."

"Number one," I said with a shocked look on my face. What an insult. I wanted to be the *only* one. Maybe I was number one in his thick black book, but at this point, I couldn't take his words seriously. "What's the special occasion?"

"The special occasion is to show you how much I appreciate you being there for me. How much I know you want to kick my ass to the curb but you don't. Also, to show you how much I enjoy being with you."

"Jaylin, I already know that. It's just sometimes my jealousy gets the best of me. Felicia doesn't threaten me in any way. Of course I don't like the idea of you being with her, but this situation is only temporary."

Even though my words were the total opposite of what I truly felt, I didn't want Jaylin to know how much his relationship with Felicia bothered me. I placed my hand on the side of his face and he kissed it.

"Sex, Nokea, that's all it is. I have very little feelings for Felicia, and you have nothing to worry about. Don't you ever forget it, all right?"

He gave me a quick kiss on the lips and I pushed Felicia's drama to the side. Jaylin grabbed his keys, but as we got ready to walk out the door, the phone rang.

"Wait a minute, baby. Let me see who that is." He walked over to the phone. "Jaylin," he answered. "No," he said, smiling. "I mean, yes, I . . . I was on my way out the door. Why don't you give me a call tomorrow?" He paused. "Hey, no bother. Just call me tomorrow and we'll talk."

Jaylin hung up, and instead of looking at me, his eyelids dropped low. I knew him too well. That was a new woman. I didn't even have to ask him. But I wasn't tripping, because if anything, she'd replace Felicia, not me.

Our time together was fabulous. Jaylin was right; The Hampshire had it going on. The staff waited on us hand and foot like we were celebrities or something. As soon as our wineglasses were empty, they'd rush over to fill them. Jaylin ordered the filet mignon and I had a juicy New York strip steak. The food was to die for, and my time with Jaylin was truly the best. As the soothing jazz played throughout the restaurant, Jaylin asked me to dance.

"You feel so good in my arms," he whispered.

"So do you, baby. I love you so much, and the thought of us being like this forever is what keeps me sane."

"Yeah, me too. Promise me something, though?"

"What's that?"

"Promise me no matter how rough things might get for us, you'll always be there. I know it's asking a lot, but you're the only good thing I got in my life. I'm very thankful for you. If I didn't have you in my corner for all these years, I don't know where I would be."

"That's an easy promise for me. I know it's going to get rough—it's already rough allowing you to do some of the things you do. But I have a reason for putting up with you. You are mine, and we were made for each other. Our parents always said we were destined to be together, so I'll wait. You'll come around, sooner than you think." I rubbed my hands up and down his back. He squeezed me tighter and kissed my forehead.

"Woman, that's why I care about you so much.

Ain't nobody like you, and one day I'm going to make you all mine."

I wanted to believe Jaylin, but I had serious doubts. His actions didn't jive with his words, and I wasn't about to get my hopes up. We wrapped up dinner and then went back to his place for a nightcap. Like many times before, I wanted to give myself to Jaylin that night, but I couldn't. I didn't want to be on the other side with Felicia and the rest of his female companions. I wanted to continue to stay in a category all by myself. In his own words, he cared for me more than anyone else. I had to believe that.

But I also hadn't forgotten about his earlier phone call. My gut signaled more trouble for us, but only time would tell.

4

JAYLIN

Damn! Scorpio called and I didn't even get a chance to talk to her last night. I was glad when Nokea left. She hung around all day today as I waited for Scorpio to call back. As of yet, she hadn't, but I was anxious to speak with her.

Stephon and one of our longtime friends, Ray-Ray, came over to watch the football game. That took my mind off Scorpio for a while, and I was glad to be focused elsewhere.

"Negro, are you going against the Rams or what?" Ray-Ray said as we debated who'd go to the Super Bowl.

"You know ain't nobody in the league better than them right now. As long as we got the baddest quarterback out there, the Super Bowl is well within our reach," Stephon said, agreeing with Ray-Ray.

"All I'm saying is we need to quit with the turnovers and get back to business. Now, ain't nobody gonna beat us. I just think we got some work to do," I defended.

"Then stop talking that bullshit. You gotta have a little confidence in them, that's all. I don't care how many damn turnovers they make, no other team in the league can beat them."

As Stephon continued to rant, I walked over to the bar and poured another glass of Courvoisier. When the phone rang, I wondered who it was. I figured it wasn't Felicia because I fucked her well yesterday, and she knew I wasn't hooking up with her again until Friday. Nokea had left earlier and said she was spending the day with her parents. I knew it wasn't any of my clients because they knew better than to call me over the weekend. And my boys were here. I hoped it was Scorpio as I rushed to answer the phone.

"Jaylin," I answered in a deep tone.

"Hi, Jaylin. Hope I didn't catch you at a bad time again."

"No, you didn't. As a matter of fact, I wondered when you were going to call back." I walked off into the other room so my boys couldn't hear me.

"I would've called you earlier, but I took my daughter to Forest Park. We usually go there to spend a little quiet time together."

Damn, I thought, a kid. I particularly didn't want a woman with kids after the way I felt when Simone took away my daughter, but maybe this would have to be exception number two for Scorpio. *If I have to make any more, she's history*, I decided.

"To Forest Park, huh? That's cool. Gotta take time out for the kids."

"So, are you in the mood for company tonight? I've been kind of thinking about you and would like to see you."

Now she was really rushing things. I thought it was my job to ask her out. But then again, wasn't nothing wrong with confidence.

"Sure, Scorpio, I would love some company tonight. What time should I expect you?"

"Is eight o'clock okay with you? All I need to do is find a sitter and I'll be there by eight."

"It's on. I'll see you at eight."

I gave Scorpio directions to my crib. I wanted to screen her a little more, but her kid was bugging her in the background. I had my doubts about this one. But, what the hell? If anything, I'd get a good fuck and call it a day.

Ray-Ray's short, roly-poly self and Stephon weren't budging. They hung around just so they could check out Scorpio when she came. I went upstairs and changed into something comfortable—my silk burgundy pajamas—and turned on a song by Frank Sinatra that played on the intercom throughout the house.

"Man, what the fuck is that?" Stephon said, laughing at the song.

"Negro, it's my 'let me come make love to you' song that be having women jumping out of their panties, that's what it is."

"Sounds more like it'll have their asses jumping out of the window to me," Ray-Ray said, giving Stephon five.

"You know, y'all really be playa-hating. I got this

nice-ass woman coming over here and you two insist on cock-blocking. Then when I put on something romantic, y'all dissing my song. I tell you what, why don't both of y'all get the hell up out of here? I'll share the gory details of tonight's events with y'all later."

Just then, we heard something that sounded like a loud truck with a rattling engine.

"What the fuck is that?" Stephon said, looking out the window.

"I don't know. I hope it ain't nobody's car," I said.

"It is a car," Stephon said, laughing. "And it's in your driveway. That pretty little thing from yesterday seems to be the owner."

"Man, what kind of fucking car is she driving?" I rushed over to the window to see for myself. This bitch had a raggedy-ass 1977 get-out-and-push Cadillac that I knew was probably dripping oil in my driveway. "Fuck that! This is it for her. I'm going right downstairs to tell her I got plans tonight and made a mistake inviting her ass over here."

"Man, now, you know you be too hard on the sistas. Everybody ain't got it like you, Jay. Give the lady a chance. She might have borrowed a car from a friend," Ray-Ray said.

"Which probably means she don't have a car at all. Man, I ain't even wasting my time."

I ran downstairs to open the door because she rang the doorbell over and over again. Ray-Ray and Stephon followed. When I pulled open the door, I opened my mouth but couldn't say nothing. Scorpio looked and smelled edible.

I moved aside and let her come in. I couldn't tell whose lip hung down the lowest—Stephon's, Ray-Ray's, or mine. She had on a white linen jumpsuit that criss-crossed in the back and tied around her neck. It draped in the front, where I could see just a sliver of her cleavage, and her long, curly hair hung on her shoulders. The bottom half of the jumper was kind of see-through. I noticed she wore a thong because of the string line on her upper hip. Her white-strapped sandals accented the outfit, and so did the red fingernail polish on her hands and feet.

"Hey, uh, Scorpio," I said, clearing my throat. "This is my cousin Stephon and one of my friends, Ray-Ray."

"Hey," both of them said in unison. They stood with pure lust on their faces. I nudged Stephon in his side to get his attention.

"Aw, wha . . . what's up, Scorpio? Nice to meet you." He reached his hand out to shake hers. She smiled and shook his hand. Stephon didn't let go. He held her hand and rubbed it with his other hand. "Smooth. Sweetie, you got some smooth-ass skin. What you putting on yourself these days to keep yourself so smooth like that?"

"No secret," she said, appearing unfazed by his comment. "I always bathe in baby oil, that's all."

"Hey, Scorpio, why don't you go ahead and have a seat? I'm gonna walk my cousin to his car."

"Okay, Jaylin, take your time."

Stephon and Ray-Ray waved good-bye to Scorpio and we walked to Stephon's car.

"Man, man, man! What you gon' do with all that in there?" Stephon said. "Sista might have a fucked-up car, but a woman like that, I'd buy her a new one. She is fiiiiine. And if she doesn't meet your expectations, then pass her to me. She definitely meets mine."

"Negro, please. I'm gonna try to tap that ass tonight, and afterward, you can have it. If it ain't Nokea, I ain't buying nobody shit. When Scorpio leaves, there better not be no oil stains in my driveway from that fucked-up car. If there is, I'm gonna ask your ass to correct it, since she'll be kicking it with you."

"That's all right with me. I'll correct anything she wants me to. But you'd better watch out. She got an interesting look about her. I think she's gonna give you a run for your money."

"Please. I've had finer women than her chasing after my ass. Trust me; she'll be calling you tomorrow."

"All right, Jay. Don't say I didn't warn you. Something about that woman just doesn't sit right with me. And brotha, please strap one on tonight. I don't want you around here burning. You catch my drift?"

"Always, my brotha, always."

"Well, Ray and me gon' go get our roll on at Skate King in Pine Lawn. Are you sure you and Miss Sexy don't wanna come along?"

"Naw, man, I'm staying right here tonight. I'll roll with y'all some other time. Besides, I ain't in no mood to see you bust your damn head open tonight. Them cats be rolling down there, and personally, I don't think you can hang."

"Hang on this," Stephon said, grabbing his dick. "I'll holla at yo' ass tomorrow."

I went back into the house and saw Scorpio in the living room, looking at a picture of Mama on the fireplace mantel.

"Is this your mother?" she asked.

"Yes, it is," I said, taking the picture from her hand. "She's dead, though. I like to keep her memory around, you know what I mean?"

"Yeah, I sure do. My mother died of cancer when I

was nineteen, and I still haven't been able to part with her pictures yet."

"So, can I get you something to drink? I haven't had time to cook any dinner because my boys had me tied up all day with the football games. Or, if you'd like, we can order some Chinese."

"I love to cook. Take me to your kitchen and I'll be more than happy to throw us a little something together."

I took Scorpio's hand and led her into my kitchen. Her eyes wandered. "Jaylin, this kitchen is immaculate. It's a woman's dream to have a kitchen this beautiful and clean. Are you sure you live alone?"

"Of course I do. I used to have a maid, but I got a few good friends who help me keep it clean every once in a while."

"Oh . . . I see. So, what do you have in the fridge?" She boldly opened it.

"I picked up some ground chuck from Straub's last week, and it's the only thing that's thawed. How about some Hamburger Helper? I got a box of cheeseburger macaroni on the shelf and it shouldn't take long at all."

I put everything on the counter for Scorpio and told her I would be back. I went to my bedroom to call Nokea back because I had seen her number on the caller ID. I guess she'd made it back from her parents' house and was calling to let me know. Surely, I didn't want her to show up tonight and mess up my action with Scorpio.

"Hey, baby, you call?" I asked as I sat on my bed.

"Yes. I just wanted to tell you what a wonderful time I had last night. It kind of got me thinking more about our relationship. How much you and I are meant for each other. How much I know you love me and I know some day you'll be my husband. So, baby, I . . . I think I'm ready."

"Ready for what?"

"I'm ready to give myself to you. I want to make love to you tonight."

After all this time, tonight she decides she's ready? I know I was anxious to get inside Nokea, but tonight wasn't the time.

"Baby, listen. I know how strongly you feel about saving yourself, and I want you to continue to stand your ground. Even if you're ready, I'm not. You're special to me, and I don't want to have sex with you while I'm involved with other females." I couldn't believe that bunch of bullshit had come out of my mouth.

"Once I give myself to you, hopefully your involvement with other females will stop. I thought you wanted this Jaylin, but—"

"I do, baby, but not while I'm having sex with other people. Tell you what; just give me some time to cut Felica loose. I don't want to make love to you until I'm free of these other women. That's fair, isn't it?"

"But—"

"But nothing, Nokea. Let me get off the phone so I can get me some rest. I'll call you tomorrow when I get off work. You can come by then and we can talk more about it."

"All right, Jaylin, but, do . . . do you have company? You seem to be rushing me off the phone."

I'd never lied to Nokea, but if I told her the truth, she'd have more questions for me. I was trying to work on getting my thang wet, and now wasn't the time for questions.

"No. I'm just tired, baby. That's all. I promise I'll call you tomorrow."

She gave me a kiss over the phone and hung up. I hated to lie to her like that, but I guess there's a first time for everything. I just hoped she believed me. I wasn't in the mood for one of her unexpected visits.

When I got to the kitchen, I could have died. Scorpio had burned the hamburger meat, and grease was everywhere on my island. This was enough for me. Bitch couldn't even cook? I didn't care how fine she was, she had to go.

"Say, why don't you go in the living room and have a seat. Let me clean up things in here and I'll call and order us some Chinese."

"Jaylin, I'm so sorry. I searched for some seasoning salt in your pantry and when I turned around, the meat had burned. Let me make it up to you. I'll pay for the Chinese if you call it in."

"Okay, whatever. Just go have a seat in the living room and I'll be out in a minute."

She walked her sexy ass into the living room and out of my presence. As I cleaned up, I tried to come up with a good reason for her to leave so I could call Nokea back and tell her I changed my mind about waiting. Right about now, I'd rather be making love to Nokea than screwing this dizzy-ass broad.

I turned off the kitchen light and walked into the living room. Scorpio was leaned back on the sofa with her arms folded and her legs crossed, humming with the music on the intercom. I sat next to her.

"Scorpio, look. I think it was a big mistake asking you to come here tonight. I, uh, have a woman, and right now, we're having a difficult time in our relationship. I thought inviting you here would ease my pain, but it's not."

"How did you intend for me to ease your pain, Jaylin?"

"I don't know. Sex, probably, but I don't think it's in my best interest to go there with you. If my woman finds out, we'll probably never be able to work things out."

Scorpio reached over and twirled her fingers through my hair. "I'm so disappointed to hear that," she said seductively. "But what makes you think she's going to find out?"

"You know how y'all women are. Sooner or later, the truth always comes out."

She leaned in to whisper in my ear. "If you won't tell, then I won't tell."

Just that fast, her lips touching my earlobe made me want to fuck her.

"So, are you saying if you let me hit that, I don't have to call you tomorrow?"

"All I'm saying is I live for today and not for tomorrow. And right now, today, I want to see what this big bulge in your pants is all about. I'd love to feel it inside of me, and I want to get to know it, just for the night. If you have no desire to call me tomorrow, then don't. I promise you I won't cry, and I doubt that I'll lose any sleep."

Sounded like a motherfucking plan to me. Scorpio stood up and removed her white sandals. I scooted back on the couch, stretched my arms out, and watched her. She stood right in front of me and untied her white linen jumper. She eased it down past her hips, until it hit the floor. When she turned around to walk over to my furry black rug, I noticed a tattoo of a red rose smack on the right cheek of her fat, juicy ass. She lay on the floor with her breasts facing me and her legs opened so I could see the neatly trimmed hairs that covered her pussy. My dick throbbed like I was about to explode. I stood up and got ready to remove my pajama pants.

"Jaylin, no," she said seductively. "Stay right there, baby. When I need you, I'll ask for you." She inserted her finger into her goodness and my eyes were glued to it. She moved her finger in and out and then licked it. I sat filled with excitement as she rolled her finger over her clitoris and her juices started to flow.

"Now, it's your turn." She opened her legs wider and invited me in.

I rose up and removed my pajamas while Scorpio anxiously awaited me on the floor. When she got a glimpse of my nine-plus inches, she smiled. My intentions were to go for the good stuff first, but I also wanted to tease her ass like she had done to me so well.

She held her finger out and I licked it to get a quick taste of her. I eased my body between her legs and placed my lips on her breasts. She sat up on her elbows and watched to make sure I did a good job. As I teased her nipples with the tip of my tongue, she closed her pretty eyes and leaned her head back.

I licked my way down her chest and rolled my tongue inside her pierced belly button. The foreplay was getting intense, and when she lay back and closed her eyes tighter, I went for it all. My face brushed against her soft, pillowy hairs and I took a few light licks up and down her moist slit. I stuck my tongue deep within, and as she moaned, I could feel her body tremble. I rolled my tongue around her clitoris and sucked the juices as they rolled down my lips. Nothing but the taste of sweet cherry lemonade hit me. When I finished, I found her lips and shared the taste with her.

"Fuck me, Jaylin," she whispered in my ear. "Fuck me good, baby." She didn't have to ask because that's what I intended to do.

I stretched her legs out in the air and held them with my hands while she lay back. I rubbed myself up against her to make sure she was soaking wet. As I entered, I damn near lost control. I dropped her legs and leaned down to gather myself for a minute. Pussy felt so warm and good on my dick, I thought it had melted. I closed my eyes and tried to think about the St. Louis Rams football game today, about my job—anything to prevent myself from coming too quickly.

I was able to maintain my composure and get back to work. I worked her insides better than I'd ever done before. Turned her over and pounded her ass like a piece of meat. And just when she thought I was finished, I bent her body over my leather sofa, held her tiny waistline, and stroked her from behind. After all, she was the one who said "fuck me."

Scorpio and I took deep breaths as we lay on the couch. My legs were open and she had her slim, sexy body on top of mine. Her head was on my chest, and I couldn't help but rub my hands on her soft ass.

"Jaylin, I haven't had sex like that in a long time. It was so good to release all that energy with you."

"Same here. I haven't felt like that in a long time either."

"So . . . where do we go from here? I know you said

you already had somebody in your life, but I kind of felt a connection between us. Tell me if I'm wrong."

I felt as if we'd made a sexual connection too, so there obviously had to be some changes in my original plans not to call her again. For now, her having a child, a fucked-up car, and no cooking skills had to be put on the back burner. "All I can say is I'd be willing to take this one day at a time. First, let me tell you I ain't for being with just one woman. I have a lot of friends—good friends—whose company I enjoy a lot. If you don't mind being a part of my world, then sure, I'd love to keep you around."

"What's the need for so many women in your life? Can't you get everything you want from just one?"

I chuckled at the thought. "Honestly, no. Everybody in my life accentuates it in a different way. It's necessary for me to have what I want, and if somebody decides to jet, I won't be left without."

"Oh, I see. So, in what ways do the other women accentuate your life? I'm sure I can fulfill many of those needs. It almost sounds like you're afraid of being left alone."

"Maybe you can accentuate my life and bring to the table everything I need, but now isn't the time to discuss it. As for me being alone . . . a man like me will never be alone. Still, I like my space and I don't want nobody in my life around the clock."

Scorpio lay quietly with her head on my chest. I got sleepy, so I suggested we go to my room for a drink. I took her hand and we moseyed up the steps.

"Jaylin?" she said, stopping me on our way up.

"Yes."

"I forgot something."

"Forgot what?"

"Sit and I'll show you."

I sat on the steps and Scorpio brought her lips to mine. She took my hand and put it between her legs so I could feel her wetness. Then, as soon as my dick gave her some attention, she swallowed it like no other sista had done before. I leaned back and enjoyed the sensation of the back of her throat.

Just as I was getting into it, she switched positions and put it on me. Stroked me so good, I couldn't think about anything else but being inside of her.

"Scorpio, damn, baby, please. Brotha tired," I said, suddenly feeling drained, which was quite unusual for me.

"Jaylin, you ain't fucking me," she whispered in my ear. "I need a man to fuck me."

I couldn't sit there like no punk who couldn't hang, so I quickly retrieved a condom from my nearby office, turned her ass over on the steps, and tore into her from behind. She held onto the banister to keep still, and her long, beautiful hair dripped with sweat. I moved her hair over and pecked down the side of her neck. When I felt myself about to explode, I held the banister with one hand and gripped her butt with my other one.

"Woman, what in the hell are you trying to do to me?"

"I'm not trying to do anything. When I got something as good as you to work with, the best of me comes out. But, Jaylin?"

"What's up?"

"You're heavy. Do you mind getting up?" She pushed me back with her body.

"Aw, I'm sorry. I was just caught up in the moment." I stood and reached down to help her up.

We went into my bedroom. She seemed amazed as she looked up at the high coffered ceiling. I could tell she was impressed. I told her I'd had an interior decorator and paid her very well for her services.

Scorpio smiled and got her sexy self underneath my covers. I thought about the mess we'd left downstairs, and I went down there to pick up our shoes and clothes and then brought them upstairs to my room. Just the thought of my place being junky upset me. I neatly laid her outfit on my chaise and put her shoes underneath it. I hung my pajamas in the closet and got in bed next to her.

Scorpio lay on her stomach, barely keeping her eyes open. It didn't take her long to fall asleep. Some of her hair covered her face, and I moved it over to the side so I could look at her. She was an amazingly beautiful woman, but I didn't know much about her. Was she really feeling me, or could I have finally met my match? I didn't see her as being gullible, but she didn't seem bothered by me mentioning other women. I hoped like hell that she wasn't a gold-digger, but if she was, she was definitely wasting her time.

I hadn't decided if I wanted to keep her in my life; then, I lifted the cover and looked at her well-shaped naked body. After getting a good look, I decided she was a keeper. She needed some work, but that wouldn't be a problem for me. I'd just have to deal with her child and add a few enhancements to her so she could fit into my circle.

5

FELICIA

Jaylin didn't even call last night. I called his house all night but got no answer. I started to pay him a visit, but I was sure Miss Homebody was probably over there. But even if she was, he usually still answered the phone, so I didn't know what was up.

Today, I went to the Galleria at lunch to buy myself something nice. After all the bullshit I put up with from Jaylin, the least I could do was take good care of myself. As soon as I walked into Macy's, I saw Nokea on her way out with a shopping bag, which looked to be filled with men's clothing.

"I see Jaylin's got his mother going shopping for him again," I said.

"Felicia, give me a break. You know I'm not trying to be anything like Jaylin's mother. Just in case you didn't notice, he is my man, and I do take good care of him."

I could have choked. How could she be taking good care of him and wasn't even satisfying his needs? "Nokea, feel free to spend all of your little money on Jaylin. If you think buying him clothes is going to keep him, my dear, you got another thing coming."

"And Felicia, if you think screwing his brains out is going to keep him, then you got another thing coming."

"Bitch, when are you going to wake up and smell the coffee? All Jaylin wants is a good woman who can fuck him like I can. You're sadly mistaken if you think he's going to settle down with you and you ain't up-ping nothing. In this day and age, that just doesn't keep a man."

"In case you want to know, I'm meeting with Jaylin about our little problem tonight. Whenever I decide to give myself to him, you are done. So, please, enjoy his strokes while they last because your last stroke is almost over."

"If that's the case, you should've talked to him about that last night when you were there. If your decision to give it up all of a sudden didn't change anything last night, then today definitely ain't going to make a difference."

"I wasn't at his place last night. When I spoke to him, he was tired. Tired of your mess, and all these other females' mess. So, as I said before, after tonight, you're history." She turned and walked away.

I hated that little preppy bitch—maybe because deep down I knew Jaylin cared about her a little more than he did me. I overheard him speaking to Stephon one day about how she meant so much to him. He even referred to her as his soul-mate. He said that if it wasn't for *her* being there for him, he would be lost. I couldn't ignore his strong feelings for her.

Maybe it was time to face reality. What if Jaylin decided to settle down with Nokea? Where would that leave me? I knew I was too good for this kind of bullshit, but I just couldn't help myself. His sex was too good for me to let go, and until I found better, I was staying put. Yes, there were more men who had it going on like Jaylin and who were interested in me. Especially where I worked. I just didn't want to go there because relationships in the workplace never seemed to work out.

I flew down Brentwood Boulevard in my Lexus thinking about what Nokea had said about giving it up to Jaylin. Now, as far as I knew, it had been me and only me for a while. Would he really be willing to end this for a virgin who obviously didn't know how to show him the ropes? The thought frustrated me.

When I got back to work, I asked my secretary to get Jaylin on the phone. She called his office, but then told me he didn't go to work today. I tried him at home and got his voicemail. *Damn, where is he?* I thought. I hadn't talked to him since Saturday morning. Normally, by now, he would've called to say hello.

Then it hit me. Nokea said she wasn't at his place last night, so that probably meant somebody else was. He wasn't calling because he had a new bitch. Every time somebody new came along, he distanced himself. Then when he realized nobody could give it to him like I could, he would dismiss the new bitch. *So, here we go again.* I was gonna have to go over there and fuck his brains out so he could get his mind back on the right track.

As a matter of fact, since Nokea would be there, we'd have a good ole time. We hadn't had one of our deep arguments in a long time, and it was well overdue. The last time I confronted Nokea was a few months ago, but she backed down easy. I'd paid Jaylin an unexpected visit, and she was there. Jaylin asked me to leave, but I wasn't doing that before I made it clear to her where things stood between him and me.

Nokea didn't even put up a fuss, but as usual, Jaylin always sided with her and chewed me out the following day. He flat out told me that if I ever made him choose, he'd choose her. His words stung, but since I was in this for one thing and one thing only, I didn't trip.

Tonight, though, I needed to know where things stood between us. I think I felt more for Jaylin than I wanted to admit. If he all of a sudden had plans to end this, then I didn't know what I was going to do. Knowing him, he was gonna stick to the same words he'd been saying for years: "Y'all know my situation. I can't be with one woman. If you don't like it, then you know what you can do." Realistically, adding Nokea to our sexual mix wasn't going to fly, and another new woman would only make it worse.

6

NOKEA

Jaylin was ending it with Felicia tonight. This was the last straw.

After seeing her at the Galleria, I stopped at the Saint Louis Bread Company on Carondelet Avenue and saw Mona, an old girlfriend of mine from college. She sat down to have a cup of coffee and Danish with me.

"So, how's everything going, Nokea? I haven't seen you in a long time."

"It's going fine, Mona. I just got a promotion and things are going well. How about you? I heard you and Carlos tied the knot."

"Yeah, we finally got married a little over a year ago. I have a little girl. Her name is Tory Marie, and she's a beauty." Mona reached in her wallet to show me a picture of her baby.

"Mona, she's beautiful. You are so lucky." I gave the picture back to her.

"So, Nokea, you haven't tied the knot yet? I know the last time we talked, you were dating that fine investment broker. Whatever happened to him?"

"He's still around. We haven't decided to walk down the aisle yet, but it's coming. Probably sooner than I think."

"Well, don't wait too long. You know we aren't getting any younger. I had to lay it on the line for Carlos. We'd been together since college, and he still wanted to play the field. I took him to dinner one night and said 'Look, brotha, it's either the streets or me.' I made it perfectly clear that when I was gone, I wasn't coming back. Two weeks later, he proposed. Sometimes a man needs a little help. He doesn't realize a good thing until it's gone. And even though he was somewhat pressured, we have a good life together. Every day he thanks me for getting him on the right track."

"I'm sure everything will work out for Jaylin and me. We've known each other a long time—and you're right, we're not getting any younger. I can't wait to have beautiful babies with him like you have with Carlos. Are you planning to have any more?"

"I sure am. Carlos wants to wait, but he doesn't know I stopped taking my birth control pills. So, I'll have another surprise for him very soon, I hope."

"Girl, you crazy. But it's good to see things are going well for you."

"Same here, Nokea. But you get that handsome man to marry you so y'all can start making those beautiful babies." She looked down at her watch. "Look, I gotta go. I have a hair appointment at three, and since I know I probably won't get out until late, I'd better get on my

way. It was good seeing you, Nokea. Call me some time."
She gave me a piece of paper with her number on it.

I watched Mona get into a brand new Jaguar. She
appeared to have it going on. Carlos had a good job
and she didn't even have to work unless she wanted to.
If she did, she had her marketing degree to fall back on.

I knew what she said was right. I couldn't put this
off with Jaylin any longer. My birthday was just two
weeks away and I'd be thirty years old. I was ready to
give myself to the man I loved. I'd had thoughts of
doing so for a very long time. Bottom line was I'd
given Jaylin nine years of my life and things hadn't
changed since day one. He'd been with plenty of other
women, and I'd put up with it simply because he
promised that some day all of it would end. How stupid could I be? I must be out of my mind to put all of
this into a relationship and not expect a marriage pro-
posal by now. Our quality time together had to be on
specific days because he had to make time for his other
women. That was ridiculous and I knew it.

I sighed deeply and thought about my stupidity. I
shouldn't have been letting him treat me that way. But
then again, maybe it was my fault for not giving myself
to him sooner. Maybe if I just did it, then we could finally take our relationship to the next level.

That prompted me to call him to make sure we were
still on for tonight. His secretary, Angela, said that he
had worked from home that day, but when I called, he
didn't answer. I supposed he had to run an errand or
something, so I headed for home to change into something more enticing to wear that night. I had a feeling
that this would be a turning point in our relationship.
I couldn't wait to give Jaylin exactly what he'd been
waiting for.

7

JAYLIN

"Mmm-mm-mm, Scorpio, you sure know how to fuck up a brotha's mind," I said, lying next to her in bed.

"I told you I can go forever, as long as I'm with someone like you."

"Well, Ms. Energizer Bunny, you just keep on going." I rolled on top of her and kissed her again.

We had been at it all day long—on the floor, in the tub, on the chaise in my room, and of course, in my bed. Time flew by. I didn't even have enough strength to get my ass up and go to work. I called Angela and told her to take messages for me today, and if anybody important called, to hit me on my private line at home. The only people who had that number were her and Stephon. Since that phone didn't ring, I spent the entire day fucking Scorpio. She just couldn't get enough of me and I couldn't get enough of her. This woman was mine, and I didn't care what anybody thought. She wasn't leaving my life anytime soon.

Scorpio got up and took a shower. I watched her through the glass door, standing with soap and water dripping down her naked body. My dick got hard again, but I was too tired to go at it. I picked up the phone and called Angela to see if anybody had called.

"Jaylin, where have you been? Are you coming in at all today?" she asked anxiously.

"Hold on, what's the problem? I told you earlier I wasn't coming in. I also told you if it was important to call me on my private line."

"It's nothing important, but your friends—I mean your girlfriends, or whoever the hell they are—been calling here like crazy looking for you. I can't get anything done if I'm interrupted by personal calls for you."

"Sorry, Angela. I'll call them in a minute. How's the market doing today?"

"Actually, it's up. Everything is looking pretty good, but you know how the market can be."

"Trust me, I know. I had a feeling that today would be a good day. That's why I stayed my ass at home."

"Negro, please. You know you stayed at home because you got some female over there. But that's your business, not mine."

"That's right, Angela, it is my business. When I was at home smacking bellies with you, you didn't seem to have a problem with it."

She laughed. "You know I'm just messing with you. But it would be nice to get things going again."

"Not a chance in hell. You're married now—to my boss' son—and we can never go there again."

"Darn. I had hoped there was something I could do to change your mind about that."

"Nothing. Now, transfer me to my voicemail so I can check my messages."

Angela transferred me to voicemail and I heard messages from both Felicia and Nokea. One of my most important clients had also called and said he wanted to buy some more shares of this company that was booming on the West Coast. That meant more money for me, so I went downstairs to my office to call him.

"Mr. Higgins, how are you, sir? I just got your message. What deed can I do for you today?"

"Jaylin, I think this fucking company is going to explode. I want to buy more shares now because when it does, buddy, I'm going to take my family and move my ass to a different country. Maybe even Africa," he said, laughing.

Ha, ha, ha. Africa my ass.

"Sounds like a plan, Mr. Higgins," I said, laughing right along with him. "I'll take care of that for you immediately. How many additional shares would you like to purchase?" Higgins gave me a figure that could help set me up even more.

I continued sucking up to him and laughed at his corny jokes. Fifteen minutes into our conversation, the door to my office squeaked open and Scorpio appeared, with only a towel wrapped around her. I put my finger on my lips, gesturing for her to be quiet. She smiled and walked over to my desk, pushing my papers aside so she could sit on it. I leaned back in my leather chair and watched as she removed the towel. I closed my eyes and tried to focus on my conversation with Higgins.

She took my hand and made me feel her insides. Getting excited, I tried to end my conversation with Higgins, but he just kept on talking. I stood up and slid my boxers down with the phone rested on my shoulder. I hurriedly inserted myself, and we rocked back and forth for a while; then Scorpio loudly added her famous words, "Fuck me, Jaylin."

Higgins cleared his throat and asked, "Jaylin, buddy, am I interrupting something?"

"No, not at all." I placed my hand over Scorpio's mouth. "That was just a friend of mine joking around with me, that's all."

"Sounds like she's doing more than just playing around with you, buddy. Sounds like she's fucking the shit out of you, or you her," he laughed.

"Well, you know how it is," I shot back.

"Why don't I just call you tomorrow? Hey, I got a better idea. Why don't we get together for a game of golf on Friday? The last time, you beat me and I owe you one."

"That's fine, Mr. Higgins. I'll see you Friday."

"Hey, Jaylin, suck on those tits for me," he said, laughing and finally hanging up.

I let the phone drop to the floor and Scorpio and I continued our midday session on my desk. It took a while for me to come because she had nearly drained me. Then, when she gave me some love and tender care with her mouth, I was forced to release myself.

I fell back in my chair and she took a seat on my lap. "Baby, that's it for the day," I said. "Don't you ever get tired?"

"Not really. I thought you were going to join me in

the shower, but when you didn't, I came looking for you."

"That's cool and all, but you can't be messing with me like that when I'm talking to my clients. Luckily, he's cool like that. Some of them be tripping when it comes to their money. They want a broker who sits in front of the monitor all day long and does nothing but watch the market go up and down."

"Sorry, but I couldn't help myself. You make me feel so good that when I want to feel you, I just got to feel you, no matter where you are."

My private line rang, so I patted Scorpio on her ass and made her get up.

"Man, why haven't you been answering your phone?" It was Stephon. "I called you at work and Angela's crazy ass told me to hit you on your private line."

"I was too tired to go in today, bro. Just wanted to lay my head down for an extra day. You know how that is."

"So, I guess that means Scorpio wore that ass out last night, huh?"

Scorpio was listening in on my conversation, so I put Stephon on hold.

"Say, baby, do you mind? I need to take this call. Why don't you go to the kitchen and find us something to eat? I'm hungry, aren't you?"

"All right. I'll try and find something," she said, walking out.

"And baby," I yelled, "don't cook nothing! Put together a salad or something."

She put her hand on her hip and rolled her eyes at me then gave me the finger.

"Now, I'll stick something up your ass if you want me to," I said, laughing.

"We might have to try that later."

She winked and walked out.

"Damn," I said, shaking my head and putting the phone back on my ear. "Yeah, man, I'm back."

"What the hell's going on over there? What's all this 'stick it here and there' stuff I hear you talking?"

"Stephon, this woman is bad! She's been over here since y'all left, wearing my ass out. I ain't never, and I mean never . . . Did I say never?"

"Yeah, you did, man."

"Never has a sista put it on me like that. She done set that shit out!"

"Damn, I knew she would be good. She had that seductive look about her that said she was capable of putting it on your ass. As soon as she walked in the door, her pussy screamed your name."

"Yeah, and it's been calling me ever since."

"My question is, what you gon' do with it? You know Nokea and Felicia ain't having it this time. They start acting funny every time you bring somebody new to the circle. And if I can recall, the last time you tried that shit, they were both about ready to kill you."

"Bro, how many times I gotta tell you I got this under control over here? I know I'm playing with fire, and you're right, the last time brought about much chaos. But it also showed me that no matter what, Nokea and Felicia ain't going nowhere. I've been with Nokea for nine years and Felicia for four. If they ain't stepped by now, they're here to stay."

"You g'on with your bad self. But, uh, I thought today you were going to be passing Scorpio to me."

"Now, I know what I said last night, but this a different day. Let me enjoy things while they last. If I get tired by next week, next month, or next year, I'll send her your way then."

"Sounds like you're gonna buy that car sooner than you thought?"

I laughed. "Yeah, I guess she would look pretty damn good in a Navigator or an Escalade, but, uh, she gotta do a little more work on me before I consider that."

"Seems like she's already moving in the right direction. She done stepped up since last night. She wasn't getting a damn thing then."

"And she still might not, but maaaan, the way she be popping that thang . . . whew! It's enough to make any man go crazy."

"You got my shit over here on the rise just thinking about it. Let me call one of my ladies so they can shake a brotha down tonight."

"You do that. I'll call you later."

When I hung up, I called Nokea. She answered on the first ring.

"Jaylin, where have you been? I was coming over to talk to you in about an hour."

"Talk to me about what?"

"About what I mentioned last night, silly. You said we could continue our conversation today."

Damn, I had completely forgotten about Nokea coming over today. Scorpio had my mind twisted. All I'd been thinking about was being in between her legs. Her sex was the best. I didn't think any woman was capable of taking in my nine-plus inches without a fight, but Scorpio had done it.

I rubbed my goatee and sucked in my bottom lip. "Nokea, baby, I'm sorry. I forgot you wanted to talk. Look, my decision still stands. I don't want you to give yourself to me right now. So, really, there's nothing for us to discuss."

"I don't care what you say. We have a lot to discuss, and I'll be over there within the hour. Tired or not, you're going to hear me out." She hung up.

I didn't call back because I heard something fall in the kitchen. I ran to see what it was. Scorpio had dropped a glass bowl on the floor.

"What are you doing?" I asked, irritated.

"It just fell, Jaylin. When I turned around, my elbow must've knocked into it and it fell."

Since she was in the kitchen with no clothes on, I helped her bend down and pick up the glass and eventually forgave her. We sat on the stools and ate the salad she'd made. I'd had better, but since I didn't have any cooked ham to jazz it up, the vegetables had to do.

I knew Nokea said she was on her way, but I wasn't going to make Scorpio leave just because Nokea insisted she wanted to talk. If anything, she knew better than to pressure me into doing something I didn't feel like doing. Out of respect, though, I explained the situation to Scorpio as she lay across my bed.

"If you don't mind, I have some company on the way. She wants to discuss some things with me, and it shouldn't take long at all. If you wouldn't mind staying in my bedroom, that would prevent me from answering any questions about us."

Scorpio sat up and placed her long hair behind her ears. She avoided eye contact with me and rubbed the tips of her manicured nails. "Is she your girlfriend?"

"Well . . ." I hesitated. "We're very close friends."

"Intimate friends?" she asked, finally making eye contact.

"No, but a friend who would trip if she knew about our actions for the past two days."

"I thought you had an understanding with your women. If she's coming over here to start any trouble, I can just leave. I don't believe in fighting over a man. No offense, but there are plenty of men to go around."

"I agree, but there's only one of me." I stood up and stretched. "Nokea ain't the kind of woman who would pick a fight either, so can I count on you to stay in my room? I'd really like for you to stay. We still have plenty of unfinished business to take care of."

"I'll stay, Jaylin, but you'd better hope things don't get out of hand. If so, you'll see a side of me that you may not like."

"I didn't know that side of you existed. Thus far, I'm digging you from every angle."

When the doorbell rang, Nokea wasn't bullshitting. She was right on time. Her face did not display a smile.

"Baby, what's up?" I said, knowing that I didn't want to be bothered.

"What's up is whose darn car is that in your driveway?" she yelled.

"Come in, have a seat, and lower your voice. I don't like you yelling at me like that. It definitely ain't your style."

Nokea folded her arms and went over to the couch. As usual, my baby looked and smelled good. She had her hair neatly layered on the sides and spiked in the front. Her sexy little blue dress showed every curve on her petite frame, and her hips swayed as she sauntered into the living room. She turned and pointed her finger at me.

"I'm not sitting down, Jaylin. I'm interested in knowing whose car that is outside!"

"For the last time, don't be yelling in my house like that. My neighbors don't need any reason to call the police. You know these folks in Chesterfield don't play. Sit down so we can talk."

She finally sat down and I sat next to her. I took her hand.

"The car outside belongs to a nice young lady that I met not too long ago. She's upstairs in my room watching TV, and she's leaving tonight."

Nokea snatched her hand away from mine. "Was she here last night when I called you? Is that why you didn't want me to come over, and why you haven't been answering your phone?"

"Because I've been busy. I had some work to do, and when I spoke to you last night, I was in my office trying to catch up."

She rolled her eyes. I could practically see the smoke coming from her ears.

"You still haven't answered my question. Was she here last night?"

I dropped my head back and looked up. "Yes, she was, but—"

Nokea pushed my face, and when I sat up straight, she smacked me. I closed my eyes and turned my head to prevent myself from fucking her up. I realized I deserved it for lying to her, so I couldn't do anything but shake it off.

She covered her face with her hands and started to cry. I felt worse than I'd ever felt before because I'd never seen her cry like that. I leaned over and wrapped my arms around her.

"Look, I'm sorry. The last thing I want to do is hurt you, but it ain't like you don't know my situation. I don't know what you want from me. For years, you've been telling me you don't want to have sex with me, and now you've changed your mind. You've been on and off, Nokea, and how do you think that makes me feel?"

She shook her head from side to side and slapped me again. "You are so full of it. You know darn well what I want, but you've refused to give it to me. This sex thing wouldn't even be an issue if you would've focused your time and energy on our relationship only. But that's asking too much of you, Jaylin, isn't it?"

I rubbed my goatee and pressed my lips together. Nokea had definitely touched a nerve by slapping me and by not understanding what I was saying.

"Look, if you say you love me like you do, then there shouldn't have been no problem with you wanting to give yourself to me. Now you expect me to drop everything and be done with it. It doesn't work like that, Nokea. This process takes time."

Nokea dropped her head on my shoulder to cry, and I felt terrible. I hated to see her like this, but nothing I said seemed to soothe her pain. "Baby, do you hear what I'm saying to you? What do you want from me? I can't change things overnight, and I'd be lying to you if I told you I would." Besides, I had no intention of dropping Scorpio any time soon now that I knew what a freak she could be.

She lifted her head and wiped her tears. "Jaylin, I love you. I've always loved you, but you have been too blind to see that all along you've had everything you've needed. Did it ever occur to you that if you gave our relationship a chance, I would eventually come around and give myself to you? Not once did you give up your women for me. I've always been in this with somebody else.

"I refuse to go on like this anymore. Some things need to change. All of my girlfriends are getting married, making commitments, and I'm still hoping for things to work out for us. I'm not getting any younger, and neither are you."

I couldn't say anything. I knew what I had put her through, but I thought she understood what a man like me needed. I got up to pour myself a shot of Martel. When the doorbell rang, I poured a double shot because I felt something heavy about to go down.

When I opened the door, Felicia walked in, Scorpio stepped out of my bedroom, and Nokea stood up next to the couch. *Damn*, I thought. *What in the hell am I going to do now?*

Since Scorpio was my new lover, all eyes were on her. She had on my black silk robe, tied so low that we could see part of her left breast.

"Who in the fuck is that?" Felicia asked.

"You know, for a woman who's supposed to be classy, your mouth is extremely foul. Chill out with that, all right?" I tried to play it cool; after all, this was my house and I was in control.

I looked up at Scorpio. "Hey, why don't you come downstairs? I want to introduce you to some friends."

As Scorpio walked down the steps, her pretty, tanned legs and private parts peeked through my robe. I know damn well Felicia and Nokea got a peek because they looked as if their insides burned with fire.

Scorpio stepped into the living room with Felicia and Nokea, who were already moments away from killing each other.

"Ladies, first let me say that I don't want no shit up in here tonight. We're going to settle this like adults, and everybody's gonna go home happy, all right?"

Scorpio had a smirk on her face. She appeared to be getting a kick out of the drama. "I heard all the yelling, so I stepped out of the bedroom to make sure everything was okay. I really don't want to be a part of this, and if you don't mind, I can just go. You've already made it clear to me where things stand with us, so there's no need for me to stay and battle it out with these two women."

Now, that was my kind of woman. She was thrilled by the drama, but she wasn't going to put me on blast in front of everyone. "Thanks, Scorpio. I appreciate you not stressing a brotha. Just leave the robe on my bed when you change."

"Of course," she said, making her way back up the steps.

Felicia cleared her throat and started working her neck. "Sorry, Mr. Rogers, but it's not that easy for me. I need to know what's up with us right now. I'm not going to play second to neither one of these bitches because I've done it long enough. When I saw Miss Homebody over there today, she said you were closing some doors in your life. I want to know if that door is supposed to slam on me. If so, I came to hear it straight from the horse's mouth."

I looked at Nokea. She didn't say a word, but a look of disgust was written all over her face. But tonight, I was standing my ground. If neither of them liked it, too bad. The world was mine, and I determined who stayed in it. At this point, I didn't think either of them were capable of stepping.

"Felicia, I'm gonna say this to you and Nokea—if she's listening. I am not going to limit myself to just one woman right now. Maybe in the future, but that is something I can not predict. I enjoy being with the both of you, and I refuse to choose one over the other. If you can't roll with that, then roll out. If you don't appreciate a brotha's honesty, then I don't know what else to say. I'm tired of repeating myself over and over again. It's starting to get very frustrating for me. So, tonight, I'll let the both of you decide. Either you're gonna roll with me or you're not. I'm not going to lose any sleep either way it goes."

There was silence. Scorpio walked downstairs with her white jumpsuit on, looking just as spectacular as she did when she came in last night. Nokea and Felicia looked at her with jealousy in their eyes as she walked over and kissed me on the lips.

"I'll call you tomorrow," she whispered then made her way to the door.

I hated to see her go, but I was sure she'd be making her way back to me soon. I turned my attention back to Felicia and Nokea.

"So, ladies, what's it going to be?" I rubbed my hands together, waiting for an answer.

Nokea didn't say anything, but as usual, Felicia was the first to open her big mouth.

"All I wanted to know is if you were ending it tonight to be with Nokea. Since you've made it perfectly clear that you're not," she said, looking at Nokea, "we might have been able to work out something. But I have a problem with this Scorpio chick. Sex has only been between you and me for some time.

I don't know if I can get with you screwing around with someone else. So, what the hell is up with that?"

"What's up is that I like her. I'd like to kick it with her like I do y'all, but it seems to be a problem all of a sudden."

"You damn right it is! It's a problem because I don't want no diseases from that bitch. If you ask me, she looks nasty, so I'm calling the shots on this one. When you're done with her, call me. Maybe I'll be there or maybe I won't. Who knows? But I don't want to hear from you as long as you're still with her. This one here," she said pointing at Nokea, "I can deal with. But that tramp who just left, I can't."

"So, in other words, the competition is getting too steep for you, huh? See ya later, Felicia, and don't let the door hit you on the way out."

Felicia tucked her purse underneath her arm and stamped her way to the door.

"Hey!" I yelled. "Don't have a change of heart tomorrow, because you know I don't play these back and forth games."

She ignored my comment and slammed the door. I wasn't bothered one bit by her departure. I knew Felicia would come running back. This time, though, I'd found a replacement for her, so it wouldn't be as easy for her to get back in.

Nokea sat on the couch with her fingernail in her mouth, staring at the wall in front of her.

"So, Miss Lady, are you a goner too?" I wasn't in the mood for any more bullshit.

"I'm not going anywhere, Jaylin. I refuse to lose you to women like them, and with our history, I know that one day you'll come around. I just hope I can deal with—"

I sat beside her and rubbed her hand. "Nokea, you understand me better than any woman I've been with. And deep down, you know how I feel. So, trust me this time. It'll all work out for the best."

She laid her head on my shoulder and closed her eyes. "I hope so, Jaylin. I truly hope it does."

My hopes weren't as high as Nokea's. There was no doubt that Scorpio would interfere, but I just wasn't ready to part ways with her yet. Her good-ass loving had me hooked. Maybe even more hooked than I was willing to admit. I hoped that tonight's events didn't compromise my arrangements in any way. Nokea seemed to be consistent with the new program, and I would bet a million dollars that, by the end of the week, Felicia would jump back on the bandwagon too.

8

NOKEA

Today would change my life forever. It was my birthday, and Jaylin had made plans to take me to Cardwell's at the Plaza for dinner. Afterward, we arranged to get a room at the Sheraton Clayton Plaza Hotel so I could finally show him how much I really loved him. It was time. And just maybe, things between us would be different now.

When I talked to him last night, he said he hadn't talked to Scorpio or Felicia. So, it was time to make my man as happy as I could, since his other women were out of the picture. He apologized for the other night and told me that he regretted the confrontation, that he never intended to hurt my feelings, and that he'd used a bad choice of words, referring to settling down with one woman. I still didn't know whether to believe him, but it was partially my own fault. After all, the choices in this relationship were really mine. I couldn't get mad at him for sleeping with other women if I allowed him to do it. If I could just hang on for a while, this drama would soon be over. Being with Jaylin was what I truly wanted.

Besides, Daddy loved Jaylin, and so did Mama. They always wanted us to be together. When I called Mama the other night and told her about what happened, she told me Jaylin was just going through a phase every man goes through. She said Daddy had done the same thing to her before he decided to settle down. And even though she insisted she was ready for some grandbabies, she wanted me to be sure about committing myself to Jaylin, and encouraged me not to be a fool.

After work, I drove to Macy's and bought a beautiful powder-blue negligee that accented my light brown skin. The front was lace and had a V-dip all the way down to the tip of my coochie hairs. The back was a thong and showed my butt that Jaylin admired so much. I bought some strawberries and cream body lotion to make sure I smelled extra fresh for him tonight. Then, I called him at work to make sure we were still on, and to thank him for the roses he had delivered to my office today. Angela answered with her usual attitude, and then she asked me to hold.

"Jaylin Rogers." It sounded like he was busy.

"Would you like for me to call you back?" I asked, knowing that I would be disappointed if he did.

"Naw, I got a minute. What's up?"

"Nothing much. I just wanted to thank you for the roses, and I wanted to find out what time you're picking me up tonight."

"You're welcome—nothing but the best for my lady. I'll see you around . . . sevenish?"

"Jaylin, are you sure you want to do this tonight? I mean, I'm ready, but I know you had your doubts before."

"I'm as ready as I'm ever going to be. I want to make sure you're ready. If not, baby, then now is the time to tell me. I've been thinking about your sexy little self all damn day."

"I'll see you tonight." I blew him a kiss before I hung up. It was good to know his thoughts were about me. I just hoped I didn't disappoint him. I'd dreamed of our moment together, and everything felt so right.

When I got home, I called the Sheraton to make sure everything was set for tonight. Jaylin had already taken care of things, but I didn't want anything to go wrong. So, I called reservations just to confirm.

I pranced around in front of the mirror in my blue negligee, hoping it was more than satisfying for Jaylin. I even called my best friend, Patricia, to get her opinion about the negligee and to get sex advice.

"Girl, whatever you wear, Jaylin will be pleased. Personally, I think he don't deserve you, but anyway—"

"I didn't ask for your negative opinion about Jaylin, Pat. I just wanted to know what you would wear to turn Chad on."

"Nothing. Chad doesn't give a shit what I put on. As long as I'm naked, he's good to go. And if I know Jaylin, he's the same way. He only cares about what's underneath."

"I know, but I want to kind of tease him a little bit . . . you know? He's been with all these women and has so much experience. I just hope I can please him. I wondered if you could share some tips with me."

"The only tip I'm going to give you is don't have sex with him yet. I ain't trying to be hard on you, but if you're having doubts about it, then why do it? All of these years, I've been so proud of you for not giving in to him. I wish there were more women like you who would wait until they get married. At the rate these men are going, nobody should be fucking."

"Well, you got that right, but I need to do this for me. If I really love Jaylin, and know deep in my heart we're going to be together, then why not?"

"I just want you to be sure, that's all. I don't know if giving yourself to him is going to change anything about him. He's got some personal issues he needs to work on, and it ain't got a damn thing to do with you."

I disagreed, but Pat was more than welcome to offer her opinion. After tonight, things would be different between Jaylin and me. After all, it seemed like he'd almost waited a lifetime for this moment to come, and nothing was going to stop it from happening.

9

JAYLIN

It was good to be off work. I rushed home and changed so I wouldn't be late for dinner with Nokea. She was so sweet. I had put all my issues with other women aside for the week just to make her happy. Felicia called and left me several messages, but I didn't call her back. I guess she finally realized that when I say something, I mean it. She walked out on me, and for now, she was staying out until I was ready.

My mind, though, had been kind of messed up. The thought of fucking Scorpio again stuck with me twenty-four/seven. I thought about her ass at work, at home, and even looked for her at the gym. She called and said she would be out of town for a few days and would call when she got back. And even though I wanted to hear from her, maybe a relationship between us wasn't going to work out. I couldn't stop thinking about her lack of cooking skills and her child, not to mention the fact that her fucked up car didn't look too good in my driveway. I wasn't looking for a perfect woman, but I at least wanted a woman who could cook.

I dropped the keys on the kitchen table and hurried to my room to change. I put on the gray suit Nokea had picked out for me at Saks Fifth Avenue and put on a crisp white shirt underneath. I left a few buttons undone so she could see my chest that she admired so much.

As soon as I put on my Rolex, the doorbell rang. I'd told Nokea I would pick her up tonight, but knowing her, she was anxious to see me and couldn't wait. I jogged down the steps with one black sock in my hand and the other on my foot.

Looking through the glass doors, I could clearly see it was Scorpio. I was pressed for time, but she was a sight for tired eyes, so I opened the door. I couldn't help but display a tiny smile.

"What brings you by?" I asked, closing the door behind her.

"I just got back in town. My daughter and I took a short vacation, and when we got back, she wanted to spend some time with my sister. I've been thinking about you, so I took this opportunity to come see you." She looked me up and down. "Are you about to go somewhere?"

"Yeah, I was. I have a dinner engagement tonight that I'm running a little late for."

"Do you mind if I stay here until you come home? I promise I'll have something sweet for you when you get back." She walked up to me and buttoned my shirt. I placed my hand over hers to stop her.

"Look, why don't I just call you tomorrow. I'd hate to keep you waiting all night long."

"So, your dinner engagement is going to take all night?" She pressed herself against me and my dick throbbed for her. I had to get to Nokea, but I was starting to think I could possibly cut our evening short and come home.

"No, my dinner engagement shouldn't take all night. I'll try to get back here as soon as I can."

Scorpio turned and walked up the stairs. She wore a shiny black leather skirt and a halter top with a string that crossed in the back and wrapped around to the front. Her black heels made her damn near as tall as me.

When we entered my bedroom, she sat on the edge of my bed, and I sat on the other side to slide on my sock. I knew time was getting away from me, so I went to the closet and stepped into my shoes. I looked for my black belt that was hidden away in the back of my closet. When I stepped out of the closet, Scorpio was already naked underneath the covers.

"You look awesome," she said. "I'm jealous because I'd love to be by your side tonight."

I would've loved that as well, but I knew it would be wrong to play Nokea on her birthday.

"I'll be back," was all I could say. I took my wallet off my nightstand and headed toward the door.

"Oh, Jaylin," Scorpio said softly. I turned, and she pulled back the covers and opened her legs so I could get a peek. "Try not to be too long. I'm anxious to feel you, and returning home early will bring you great rewards."

I walked over to the bed and leaned down to kiss Scorpio's lips. She aggressively pulled me down, and I eased my body on top of hers. Her body was so soft like Charmin. My hands wandered all over her, but when my dick got hard, I quickly hopped up.

"I'll be back as soon as I can, all right?"

She nodded and I left.

Nokea opened the door, looking amazing. I had stopped thinking about Scorpio at home in my bed so that I could give Nokea the attention I thought she truly deserved. She always presented herself as a classy woman. Tonight, she wore a peach stretch dress that hung off her shoulders. Her short cut was neatly lined, and her makeup had been perfectly done. Her beautiful round eyes shone when she saw me come through the door.

"Hello," she said, wrapping her arms around my waist. "You look handsome."

"You look beautiful too. Turn around so I can get a good look at you." All I could think about was taking off her dress tonight.

"So, are you still taking me to Cardwells?"

"Yes, but I want a kiss before we go."

Nokea smiled and gave me a few short pecks on the lips. She redid her M·A·C lip gloss, and then we left.

While driving down Interstate 70, my mind wandered back to Scorpio. She had it going on. When I visualized the prettiness between her legs, I licked my lips. I wanted to fuck her so badly, and thoughts of it made my dick hard.

Nokea reached for my hand. "Did you hear me?" she asked.

"No, I . . . I didn't. What did you say?"

"I said you're driving awfully fast. We're going to get there, okay?"

I chuckled, but no matter how hard I tried to focus on my conversation with Nokea, I couldn't. I drove to the lake, and after realizing I was an hour away from St. Louis, I knew there was no way in hell I would make it back to Scorpio before the night was over. I parked my car by the dock and we got out.

"Jaylin, what is this?" she said, looking at the double-deck party boat surrounded with lights and a sign that read HAPPY BIRTHDAY.

"Come on." I took Nokea's hand. "Let me show you."

Nokea and I stepped on the boat. The top deck had a table set with fine china, wineglasses, and a vase of flowers in the middle. I had even gone to the extreme of hiring some musicians from Freddy's Jazz Club in town to play some soothing music while we ate dinner. Nokea looked like a kid in a candy store. When I escorted her to the bottom deck, she opened her mouth wide. The room was lit with scented candles, giving it the smell of a flower garden; the bed had rose petals spread all over the gold satin sheets. There was a teddy bear on the bed with a T-shirt that read: *Happy Birthday! Yours forever, Jaylin*. She picked up the bear and held it close to her chest.

"Jaylin, I don't know what to say. I thought you made reservations at the Sheraton."

"I did. But at the last minute, I changed my mind. I wanted to do something special for you. I told you before how much I appreciate you being there for me, didn't I?"

"Yes, but I didn't expect this. This is way too much."

"Not for you, baby. You mean a lot to me, and this is nothing. Now, put that bear down so we can eat. I'm starving."

We both knew what the night had in store for us, so dinner was rushed. We slow danced through a couple of songs, and as I held Nokea's sexy little body in my arms, I told her how much she meant to me and apologized for any headaches I'd caused.

Moments later, I dismissed the jazz players and the waiters because it was time to get down to business. I hadn't had no loving in a little over a week, and I was ready to release this tension I had built up inside me.

Nokea took my hand and led the way to the lower level.

When we got there, she didn't waste any time. She laid me back on the bed and stuck her tongue deeply into my mouth. She unbuttoned my shirt and reached down to remove my belt.

"I'll be back," she whispered, and then walked to the bathroom in the far corner.

I took off my clothes then got underneath the gold sheets and waited for her. My dick climbed, and when Scorpio crossed my mind again, it was on full rise. I fantasized again about being between her legs, and wondered how long she'd wait at my house for me.

When Nokea stepped out of the bathroom, I turned my head and my thoughts quickly changed to her. She was one sexy woman, and through the lace in her negligee, I could see her hard nipples and trimmed coochie hairs.

"Do you like?" she said, easing her strawberryfragranced body on top of me. "I bought this just for you. I hope you enjoy taking it off me."

A satisfied smile covered my face. I laid her back so I could get on top and take control. I'd been with many virgins before, so I knew how to handle things in order to keep the rhythm flowing. I eased down her negligee and drew her breasts into my mouth. As I sucked those, she could barely keep still, so I knew when it came time for me to lick her insides, she would have a fit. And that she did. Her legs squeezed my head so tight that I could barely hear. I held her down to keep her still. My purpose was to soak her insides so it would be easier for me to enter. But as I gently went in, she got tense and backed up.

"Jaylin, I'm sorry. It . . . it doesn't feel right." Her words sounded painfully strained.

"Baby, just relax," I whispered. "I know it hurts, but you gotta help me do this."

Nokea took a deep breath and I teased her walls with the head of my dick. I inched my way in, but the warmth of Nokea's insides made me think of Scorpio. I squeezed my eyes together and tried to stay focused. Nokea, however, stopped me again.

"Jaylin, you're hurting me." She pushed me back. "Please stop. I can't take this."

This time I was upset. I couldn't get my shit off like I wanted to, or for that matter, how I had planned to. Only half of my nine remained inside, and I tried to reason with her.

"Baby, I've waited so long to feel you like this, and you've got to let me finish."

Nokea gave me a blank stare and slowly nodded. I wrapped her legs around my back, and as I started to stroke her, she grabbed my hips. I couldn't go any easier than I already was.

"If you could just stand the pain after a few more strokes, everything will be cool," I whispered.

I gave Nokea a couple more inches of me, and her fingernails pinched my skin. She wiggled her legs from my shoulders and dropped them on the bed.

"Baby, I can't," she said tearfully. "Take it out, all right?"

I stopped my motion and stared down at Nokea.

"I'm almost there. It's opening up for me, and the pain will go away."

Nokea moved her head from side to side. "You're way too big for me, Jaylin. I just can't take that kind of pain right now."

I let out a deep sigh and felt my dick deflate inside of her. Nokea apologized and backed away from me. She rushed off to the bathroom and closed the door. Fuck it! If I had gotten my shit off with Scorpio before I came, I would've been all right. This was bullshit and Nokea knew I was pissed. I couldn't believe that I'd waited years and years for this. Wasn't shit I could do but try again later.

Nokea came out of the bathroom with an embarrassed look on her face. I didn't want her to feel embarrassed about not being able to hang with me, because little did she know, there weren't too many women who could handle my length and thickness.

I patted the spot next to me. "Come here, baby. Come lay down with me. At least let me hold you."

Nokea lay next to me and rested her head on my chest. "Please forgive me," she said. "I had no idea it would be so painful. I know you're disappointed, but I—"

"Shhh . . . no need to apologize. We have to start somewhere, and I really didn't expect to get that far. But at least I got to taste you."

"Yeah, that was wild. Kind of felt good too."

"Shit, the way you squirmed around, it was better than good."

She laughed and leaned in for a kiss. I scrolled my fingertips on her back and we lay silent for a while.

"I love you, Jaylin. I love you so much."

Unable to say those words, I responded, "And you know how I feel."

Nokea had crashed out, but I couldn't sleep. My thang wouldn't go down as I thought about Scorpio at my house. It was two o'clock in the morning. I hoped she was still there waiting for me. I quietly went into the bathroom, took a shower, and tried not to wake Nokea. When I came out, I tripped over an ice bucket on the floor and awakened her. She sat up and yawned.

"Are you okay?" she asked. "Why are you dressed?"

"Baby, Stephon called and said he had car trouble. He's several miles down the highway on Interstate 70 and Lindbergh, so . . . I'm gonna go help him out. I'll be right back."

"Do you need me to go with you?"

"No, no. Go ahead and go back to sleep. I'll be back before you know it."

"Be careful."

"I will."

I flew down Highway K and took the quickest route to Chesterfield. I unlocked the door and ran upstairs to my bedroom. When I opened the door, I was happy to see that Scorpio was still there. She lay on her stomach in a deep sleep. I yanked off the covers and gazed at her naked body. Then I took off my clothes to do what I'd been thinking about all night. I eased myself into her from behind and felt instant relief. She flinched a bit and woke up.

"It's about time," she said, getting into position on her hands and knees. "I thought you forgot about me."

"Not a chance in hell, baby," I whispered. "Not a chance in hell."

10

FELICIA

I tossed and turned all night. It was damn near six o'clock in the morning and I was up thinking about that son of a bitch, Jaylin. I was furious he hadn't returned my phone calls. I tried to forget about him, but when I invited this brotha over from the past, I realized how much Jaylin really meant to me. Sex was horrible. Only lasted for about three minutes and wasn't even worth my time.

I had even given this brotha at work my phone number. Our conversation was cool, but when he told me he was married, I cut him short.

I missed the hell out of Jaylin. Friday nights were supposed to be our night, and when I didn't hear from him last night, I was really disappointed. I remembered it was Nokea's birthday, so I figured he was probably with her. When I drove by his house last night, Scorpio's raggedy-ass car was in his driveway. The funny thing was, his car wasn't there. I thought maybe it was in the garage, but when I got out and peeped inside, the only thing I saw was his motorcycle and his red Porsche Boxster.

Throughout the night, I called his house several times but got no answer. Yes, it was Nokea's birthday, but I still expected to hear from him.

I called his house again and left a nasty message on his voicemail. I decided to call his cell phone again, and after a few rings, a female answered.

"Hello," she said in a sleepy voice.

"Is Jaylin there?" I snapped.

"Who is this?"

"Just put Jaylin on the phone."

"Is this Felicia?" Nokea asked.

"Yes, it is. But bitch, I didn't call to talk to you. Put Jaylin on the phone. I have to ask him something."

"Felicia, Jaylin doesn't want to talk to you. Besides, he isn't here. Why are you calling him anyway? I thought you didn't want to have anything else to do with him."

"Don't worry about why I'm calling him. That ain't your business. I know you thought he was all yours, but there's been another change in plans. You'll never have him to yourself. N-E-V-E-R."

Nokea snickered. "Felicia, you are so wrong. I don't know when you're going to wake up and smell the coffee. Jaylin and I spent a wonderful night together. Since you walked out the other night, we've done nothing but show each other love. As a matter of fact, we spent the entire night on a boat to celebrate my birthday. Just a few more weeks of this and I'll soon be

Mrs. Rogers. So, my dear, it's really time to move on. Why don't you go find somebody else to lay you? Jaylin now has me for those intimate moments, so your services are no longer needed."

Nokea had me upset, but I wasn't going to let her know she had touched a nerve.

"Oh, you'd better enjoy your fame and fortune while it lasts. I'll be back. You can bet your life on that. And when I do see Jaylin again, I'll be sure to call you and share the details. In the meantime, you need to be worried about that other bitch that's got his ass all wrapped up. If you claim he was with you last night, then what the hell was her car doing at his house? Don't flatter your fucking self thinking he doesn't have anyone in his life but you. I find it quite sickening that you're the one who he keeps stepping on like a piece of trash. Not me, and damn sure not that new bitch." Nokea was silent. "So, Miss Homebody, I've argued with you long enough. Give Jaylin the phone, would you?"

Nokea hung up. I called back to check her for hanging up on me, but she wouldn't answer. I couldn't believe I was up this early in the morning tripping with her. He was probably lying right there and had her doing his dirty work for him.

I also couldn't believe she had given herself to him. She was probably so desperate to keep him that she thought of it as a last resort. Even though I hated the bitch, I kind of felt sorry for her. She had no clue what she'd gotten herself into with Jaylin. As a matter of fact, I was discovering that I didn't either.

11

NOKEA

I was worried because Jaylin hadn't made it back yet, and what Felicia had said weighed heavy on my mind. Like always, I reached for the phone to call Stephon to see what was up. When a chick answered, I was about to hang up, as I thought I had the wrong number. Instead, I asked for him.

"Who's calling?" she asked with a slight attitude.

"This is Nokea. I'm Jaylin's girlfriend."

"Aw . . . okay. Hold on a second, Nokea, let me wake him up."

Several seconds later, Stephon got on the phone. "Yeah," he said in a raspy tone.

"Stephon, I'm sorry to bother you, but have you seen Jaylin? He left this morning and said he was on his way to get you because you had car trouble."

"Yeah, I saw him. He left, though."

"What time did he leave?"

"Shit, uh, I . . . I can't remember. Not too long ago, I think."

"What's not too long ago? An hour ago, two hours ago? When did he leave?"

"He left about an hour ago."

"So, where did he meet you at?" I said, pressing some more.

"Nokea, look, I'm tired. You calling here with all these questions and I just got in the bed. He didn't meet me anywhere. We worked on my car in my driveway, okay?"

"Okay, Stephon. Sorry to bother you. Thanks for your help."

"You're welcome. And I didn't mean to get upset with you, but it's early and I'm tired."

"I understand. Thanks again." I hung up.

I knew the moment Stephon opened his mouth that he was covering up for Jaylin. He tripped when he said they worked on his car at home. Jaylin told me his car stopped on him right down the highway.

I got out of bed and put on my clothes. I didn't have a car, but I did have money for a taxi. The dispatcher said they'd send one right over. I sat on the bed and racked my brain. What if Jaylin lied to me? There was no way he would disrespect me like that just to be with someone else. It didn't make sense that he would go through all this trouble to get me in bed, then go home and be with somebody else. Just didn't seem like something he would do.

Before the taxi came, I called his house a couple of times, but there was no answer.

When the horn blew, I grabbed my purse and my teddy bear and left. The ride was long; the taxi driver drove extra slow down Highway 40, and the meter added up. I laid my head back on the seat and closed my eyes.

I thought about Jaylin trying to make love to me last night. His touch was so gentle, but his dick was just too much for me. I'd touched it before, and even made it grow with the stroke of my hand. Having it inside of me was so much different. I never thought it would be so painful. It had, however, made me extremely wet. No wonder all these women were going crazy over him. The way he sucked my breasts and licked my insides made me want him even more. We'd just have to take our time, though. He said he'd be willing to give it another try, as long as I was. For now, I had to find out where he'd gone and why he'd left so abruptly.

The taxi was on Chesterfield Parkway, right around the corner from Jaylin's house. My stomach felt queasy. I had a feeling something wasn't right. When the driver pulled in front of his house and I saw Scorpio's car in the driveway next to Jaylin's Mercedes, I damn near died. I paid the driver and got out of the car.

I paced myself to the door. It was unlocked, so I went inside. I quietly closed the door behind me and stood in the spacious foyer. There was no sign of Jaylin downstairs. That probably meant he was upstairs— most likely in his bedroom.

I walked up the steps and heard laughter. I also heard water and loud, satisfied moans.

My heart raced as I stepped into the bedroom. His bed was empty, but when I looked into his bathroom, I couldn't believe my eyes. Jaylin and Scorpio were in the shower. He had her pinned against the marble tile and was taking deep strokes inside of her. They were so into each other that they didn't even notice me standing in the doorway. Scorpio had her legs wrapped around his waist, and ran her fingers through his coal black, curly hair. The hot water sprinkled down on their naked bodies, and steamed filled the room. I could only see Jaylin's backside, but from the sounds he made and the dirty talk between them, I could tell he was enjoying himself.

Scorpio faced the doorway with a pleased look on her face. She kissed him like she was out of her mind, and dropped her head back with a sigh of relief.

"Your dick feels damn good inside of me. I love this dick, Jaylin. Don't you love the way this pussy feels too?"

Filled with excitement, he could barely strain the word "yes" from his mouth, but then added "hell yes." Scorpio lifted her head, and her eyes connected with mine. She opened her eyes wider and pushed Jaylin back.

"What's the matter, baby?" I heard him ask as she continued to look in my direction. He snapped his head to the side and got a glimpse of me standing tearfully in the doorway. He lowered Scorpio's legs, wiped the water off his face, and turned off the water.

I turned my back and stepped away from the doorway. I felt myself about to lose it, and covered my mouth with my hand.

Scorpio came out of the bathroom first, naked. She walked right past me as if I weren't even there. Jaylin came out with a towel wrapped around his waist and tossed Scorpio a towel to cover up.

"Would you mind going downstairs so I can talk to Nokea for a minute?"

She wrapped the towel around her body and grinned at me on her way out. Jaylin stood in front of me and tried to explain. "Nokea, I know what you're thinking, but it ain't even like that. I came here because—"

I stopped him. My chest heaved in and out. I felt like I wanted to throw up.

"This is over," I blurted out. "How could you do this to me, Jaylin? I did nothing—I mean nothing—to deserve this. What did I ever do to you but love you?"

He looked down at the ground, and then stared deeply into my eyes. "Nothing. I've always said this was my problem, not yours. But I also said that times would get challenging for us, didn't I? Please don't be upset with me. I just need time, baby, that's all. Time to sort through some—"

"Time isn't what you need. I've given you nothing but time! You have a serious problem with committing yourself to me, and I will no longer be there for you. To hell with you, Jaylin. I regret wasting all this time with you." I swiftly pushed by him and stormed out of his bedroom.

On my way out, I saw Scorpio in his bonus room, with her legs folded up on the couch like it was her darn house or something.

Jaylin came out of his bedroom and called my name, but I ignored him.

"All right then, Nokea! Have it your way, baby! Remember, though, if you walk out on me, you walk out for good!"

I slammed the door on my way out. I walked to the

BP gas station on Olive Street Road and called Pat to come pick me up. She said she was on her way. I sat on the curb in front of the gas station and cried like a baby. I cried so hard that a man stopped and asked if I needed a doctor. I declined, but I held my stomach in pain. By the time Pat came, she had to get out of the car to help me get in. My body was numb and I shook like a leaf.

"What happened?" Pat asked anxiously. "Calm down and tell me what happened." She drove off.

"You were right," I sobbed. "But I just didn't want to listen."

"I know I was right, but calm down and tell me what happened."

"He left me early this morning." I wiped my tears. "He left me so he could go home and screw this new chick he's been seeing. I had just given myself to him and everything."

"Nokea, you're bullshitting, right? Are you telling me he had sex with you and then went home to have sex with her?"

"Yes. He wasn't able to perform like he wanted to with me, so he made up a lie about going to help Stephon with his car. In reality, he went home to be with her."

"Now, that's a dirty son of a bitch! You don't even need him in your life if he's going to treat you like that. I can't believe Jaylin. I could just take my ass around to his house and give him a piece of my mind." Pat made a quick U-turn.

"Pat, please. Don't go over there. I don't want him to see me like this. I just want to let it go and move on with my life. I don't have anyone to blame but me. I made him believe that for many years it was okay for him to dump on me like this. For God's sake, that's all he knew how to do. How can I get mad if I was the one in control of my own happiness?"

Pat shook her head. "Yeah, you're right, sweetie, but you deserve so much better. And if I can help in any way by hooking you up with some of Chad's friends, let me know. They ask about you all the time, and I'd love to hook you up with one of them."

I wiped my eyes and chuckled. My best friend always seemed to have the right answer, and I hated like hell that I hadn't listened to her advice before. Maybe it was time for me to meet someone else, and making myself available was the best thing I could do.

12

JAYLIN

Scorpio and I sat up on my bed, ate popcorn, and watched the Lifetime channel. Snacking in my room and watching a channel that was made for women was definitely not my style, but I went with the flow. I laid my head on her lap and she twirled her fingers around the curls in my hair.

"Jaylin, I think I'm falling in love with you already. I can't go a day without thinking about you, and when I'm with you, I forget about the outside world."

Now, she was really rushing things. How could you love somebody and know so little about them? This was strictly a fuck thing for me, and love could not, should not, be entered into the equation.

"One day at a time, all right? I mean, I got some deep feelings for you too, but let's not go talking this love stuff yet. Besides, as you can see, I already got a full plate right now."

"I know, but you can't tell me that you don't think about me more than any other woman you've been with. We have a connection. It's not only the sex, either. Like now, I feel like I've been here with you before."

I sat up and looked at her. "I'm not saying I don't feel different about you, but this love talk got to stop. Can't we just enjoy ourselves without the hassles of a loving relationship? Hell, I don't know nothing about you. I don't know where you live, don't know what you do for a living, and don't even know how old you are. I do know that your sex be off the chain, but honestly, that's it. Women always talking about love, but give me a reason to love you, that's all I'm saying."

"Oh, I can give you several reasons to love me. But first, if you want to know more about me . . . I live in Olivette, I'm a playwright who's starving to write some new material, and I'm twenty-eight years old. When you do get to know me better, you'll eventually love me because I'm sweet, I'm very kind, and I definitely know how to please my man."

I wanted to get to know Scorpio better. At this point, giving her a chance to show that she was worthy of being more than just a sex partner wasn't going to hurt a thing. "All right, Miss Playwright, sit up here and tell me a story."

Scorpio straddled my lap with her beautifully curved, plump titties staring me right in the face.

"Well," she said with a smile, "there was this sexy, fine-ass brotha who just couldn't get enough of this woman who had come into his life and changed his whole world around. She made love to him over and over and over again, until one day, she got tired. He was afraid to love her back, and eventually she left him."

"Cut," I said, putting my hands on her waist. "It's not that I don't want to love you, Scorpio. It's just that I don't know much about love. Like I said, no woman has given me enough of a reason to love her. If you give me a reason, then maybe I'll figure this shit out. Right?"

Scorpio didn't respond. She leaned forward and gave me a peck on the lips. I knew she probably wanted more, but for now, it was strictly a fuck thing for me.

Scorpio left late Saturday night. Before I let her go, I went up in her about three more times that day. I was getting so accustomed to her, I hadn't really thought much about my situation with Nokea or Felicia. I guess it helped that Scorpio hadn't mentioned them either. I was so glad that she seemed to be a woman who didn't let my relationships with others intimidate her.

Sunday was my day. I wanted to be alone. I was tired—exhausted from all the female setbacks—so I took time for myself. I drove to C&K Barbecue on Jennings Station Road and gobbled down a tripe sandwich that I'd craved. Then I drove by North Oaks Bowling Lanes on the corner of Natural Bridge and Lucas and Hunt to see if Stephon and my boys from the barbershop were hanging out. Since I'd moved to Chesterfield, I missed hanging with the fellas, so every opportunity I got, I made my way back to the hood.

Since Stephon was nowhere to be found, I went back home and cleaned my house until it was spotless.

Scorpio had left a towel here and there, which had me a little upset. I cleaned off the desk in my office and vacuumed the carpet throughout the house. My kitchen took up the most time. I mopped the floor and wiped down the stainless steel appliances. There were a few dishes in the sink, so I knocked those out too.

By early evening, I went into my bonus room and played a game of pool. The thought of calling Nokea to apologize crossed my mind, but I didn't feel like hearing her cry again. I felt kind of bad about what had happened, but I needed so much more than what Nokea was offering. I didn't want to settle, and I wasn't going to pretend that I was happy just to spare her feelings.

Felicia had been bugging the fuck out of me. I ignored her calls because I wasn't ready to patch up things with her yet. Scorpio left a message too, saying that she was thinking about me. As hard as I tried not to, I was thinking about her too. I was starting to catch some deep feelings for her—feelings that I hadn't had for any woman other than Nokea. I worried that my feelings were a bit premature, especially since I knew so little about her. I thought about the way she be putting it on me. Even thought about what she said about me. She said she would tear down my walls and make me love her. The only person who I thought might be a little deserving of my love was Nokea. But since she didn't want to hang around and find out, what the hell?

My private line rang in my office. It was Stephon. "Say, man, you busy?" he asked.

"Nope. Just sitting around chilling, that's all."

"You don't sound too good, my brotha. What's ailing you?"

"Shit . . . nothing. Just beat. Ready to get back to business tomorrow. The Stock Market been tripping, and it got some of my clients worried."

"I know how that is because I'm losing money in that motherfucker too. But the purpose for my call is to tell you I had a visitor today."

"Who?"

"Nokea. She stopped by and apologized for calling me early yesterday morning."

"Calling you for what?"

"She called looking for you, and I didn't know what to tell her. She said you told her you were coming to help me fix my car, and I didn't know what the fuck she was talking about. I covered for you, but I really didn't know what to say."

"Man, I'm sorry. I forgot to call and tell you what to say just in case she did call. My mind was so fucked up, I didn't know whether I was coming or going."

"Well, all I wanna know is, did you really play her like that? She was in tears over here telling me about what happened. I kind of felt sorry for her."

"Negro, please. I didn't play nobody. Nokea knew what time it was. She fucked around that night, so I left. Came home and got some from a for-real woman. Now she's running over there telling you about it. Man, I tell you, women be doing some fucked up shit."

"Yeah, they do, but I ain't never seen you diss her to that level. This Scorpio chick must be a bad motherfucker."

I laughed. "As a matter of fact, she is. I kind of like her ass too."

"You like that pu-tain she be whippin' on you. I had a chick set me out like that before, and at times, I still think about her. But it was over before it started. She got all demanding and shit. Wanted me to fuck her all the time and I couldn't. You remember that chick named Claire, don't you?"

"Yeah, I remember, but I thought the reason you stopped seeing her was because she got married."

"Yeah, that's right. And I got my feelings hurt too. All I'm saying is take it easy with this chick. I have one other question for you too."

"What's that?"

"Is she worth losing Nokea over? That gal's been in your corner for a long time."

"Stephon, you know better than I do how tight Nokea and me are. She's playing that role right now, but she'll have a change of heart in a couple of days."

"For your sake, I hope so, because today when we talked, she seemed pretty confident that it was over."

"Confident, huh? Did she tell you I tried to make love to her on her birthday?"

"Naw, man, you lying. She finally let you tackle those panties?"

"Yep, that's how I know she ain't going nowhere."

"How was it, dog? Was it everything you expected it to be?"

"It was all right, man. You know how it is when you dealing with a virgin. I'm too old for that 'let me train you how to fuck me' shit, but I was willing to do it for her, so it was cool."

"Cool, huh? I don't know what you're going to do, but I got your back if you need me."

"Thanks, cuz, I'll call you later."

"Holla back," Stephon said and hung up.

I sat in my office for a while and played solitaire on my computer. I couldn't concentrate, as I thought about what Stephon said about Nokea.

I picked up the phone to call her, wanting to see why she had gone to Stephon's house to dump on me. Who was I fooling? I was actually calling because I hadn't heard her squeaky little voice today. When I dialed her number, a recorded voice answered.

"We're sorry, the number you have dialed has been changed. At the customer's request, the new number is not listed." I hung up and tried again. I thought I'd dialed the wrong number.

Again, "We're sorry, the number . . ."

Damn, she'd gotten her number changed already? Was she that upset with me that she didn't even want to talk? I thought about going to see her so we could discuss our unfortunate situation, but not today. I'd give her time to cool off and then see if I could persuade her to forgive me. Hopefully, that wouldn't be too hard.

13

FELICIA

Now, Jaylin was really pissing me off. My phone calls weren't working, so I decided to make my way to his office today. Clowning or not, I needed to know where things stood between us. I knew what I said the other night, but I missed the hell out of him. Missed his touch, his kiss, and of course, his loving. I put my braids into a bun, threw on my gray DKNY jogging suit, and my white DKNY tennis shoes. I left my jacket open so he could see my bare midriff and my orange sports bra underneath. I wanted to pretend like I'd been to the gym working out because Jaylin loved a woman who kept herself fit and trim.

I got off the elevator on the ninth floor of the Berkshire's Building, and went to the water fountain to splash water on me like I'd been working hard. I walked through the lobby and found myself standing in front of that bitch, Angela.

"May I help you?" she said, knowing damn well who I was, and who I was there to see.

"Don't play with me, bitch. You know who I'm here to see."

"Do you have an appointment?" She tried to sound professional, but she wasn't nothing but a two-dollar ho.

"Angela, I'm going to say this as nicely as I can. . . . Bitch, call Jaylin and tell him I'm here to see him."

She rolled her eyes and called him.

"He said have a seat; he'll be out shortly."

"Thank you," I said sharply then walked over to one of the leather chairs to wait.

Jaylin came out with one of his clients, smiling as he shook the man's hand. He looked scrumptious in a dark blue Brooks Brothers suit with a cream-colored shirt underneath and some dark-blue-and-cream, square-toed shoes to match. His hair looked like it had just been freshly cut, his thin beard was trimmed to perfection, and the goatee he wore fit his chin well.

I stood up as he looked at me with his catlike gray eyes, and he motioned for me to come back to his office. He stopped and told Angela to hold his calls. She nodded and cut her eyes at me.

Jaylin closed the door behind us and walked around his desk to sit in his chair. The first thing I did was look around to see if the gold pen set I'd purchased for him from Things Remembered was still on his desk. He'd always kept it on display, but now I didn't see it.

"So, what's up, Felicia? Why you bugging, baby? If my memory serves me correctly, you said you were finished with my black ass, didn't you?"

"Where are my pens at, Jaylin?"

"Cut with the bullshit, Felicia. You didn't come all the way over here to talk about no damn pens. What do you want?"

"Jaylin, calm down. I know you ain't trying to act a fool up in here, are you?"

"You got one minute to state your business. After that, I'm calling security. So, go," he said, looking at his diamond Rolex.

"All right, look. I'm sorry about the other night. I was wrong for trying to give you an ultimatum like that, but I was upset. From now on, who you see is your business. I don't care to know about your other women; just keep them far away from me.

"All I'm saying is I miss you. I miss what we shared on Friday nights, and I want to know if you wouldn't mind having me back in your so-called world."

Jaylin glared at me from across his desk and remained silent. Of course I wasn't going to put up with another woman being in the picture, and if Scorpio was going to remain in his life, Jaylin and her both were going to catch hell from me. For now, though, I had to say whatever to get my man back.

He rubbed his fingers across his lips and slowly stroked his goatee. "Felicia, you don't miss me. You don't miss a damn thing about me. That is, of course, with the exception of my big dick. Go ahead, tell me . . . and be honest. That's what it is. You miss my dick, don't you?"

"No, Jaylin, that's not it. I really miss what we had. We shared something special, just in case you can't remember."

"Something special? Yeah, I've been hearing that shit a lot lately. We ain't got nothing special, Felicia.

All we've ever had was a fuck thang, baby. I like to take good care of my fuck thangs, so that's why every once in a while we go do something special. You see, there are those famous words again: *something special.* Don't get confused. There really ain't a damn thing special about it."

"So, what are you saying? I've wasted my time coming here? Listen, do you want to do this or not?"

"You wanna do this, Felicia?" He pulled a condom from his drawer and got out of his chair. "You really want to do this? Come on, baby. Let me fuck you. That's what you came here for, so let's just get it over with." He removed his belt and unzipped his pants.

"Jaylin, no, stop!" I pulled myself away from him as he tried to lower my sweatpants. He grabbed my face and kissed me hard on the lips. I smacked his face, but he didn't flinch. He must've known that I was turned on by his aggressiveness. When he reached over and turned off the lights, I was turned on even more. He lifted me on his desk.

"Felicia, don't you ever walk out on me again. If you do, you will never, and I mean never, be able to come back to me." He forced himself inside me.

The feel of him was too good to turn away, and the only reply that I could offer was, "I will never be that foolish again. I promise you I won't."

I felt like a million dollars leaving Jaylin's office. There was no way in hell for me to allow another woman to come in and take what was mine. Scorpio had a good fight awaiting her. I wasn't about to give up Jaylin so easily.

When I passed Angela on my way out, she tooted

her lips and rolled her eyes again. I'm sure she knew sex was on the agenda, because when she knocked on the door, Jaylin hadn't answered.

"See you later, bitch," I said as I exited with my leather Coach purse clutched to my side. I went home, took a shower, and drove to the office to get something else accomplished for the day. First order of business was to figure out how I could make Scorpio and Nokea disappear.

14

NOKEA

I was miserable not talking to Jaylin, but I knew there was no way I would go back to him. My girl Pat would kill me, and so would Mama. I told Mama about seeing Jaylin with another woman and for the first time, she was disappointed. What I didn't tell her was that I gave myself to Jaylin that night. Had she known, she would have died.

She basically advised me to get on with my life and encouraged me to meet somebody new, and that's what I intended to do. I had changed my number so Jaylin wouldn't be able to reach me with another one of his lies. In fact, I even thought about moving, but I knew that would be taking things to the extreme. Since I had just gotten a promotion, I dedicated my time to my new career.

I was the new sales director for Atlas Computer Company and had to show my colleagues they had chosen the right person. It wasn't easy to do. During my first presentation, thoughts of Jaylin and Scorpio kept coming to my mind. I didn't know how I could compete with a woman who gave him so much sexual pleasure. She seemed to have the right moves, and it was just a matter of time before she worked her way into Jaylin's heart. I thought his heart belonged to me, but boy, was I wrong. I'd never seen him so anxious for a woman. For her to be around for such a short period, she was already causing a major impact.

I was so glad when my presentation was finished so I could go somewhere and get a grip on myself. No matter how hard I tried to stop the tears, they kept on coming; late at night, early in the morning. I even cried at lunch with a few of my coworkers today. They asked me what was wrong and I told them my grandfather had passed away in Mississippi. Since he'd died years ago, I felt like I hadn't burned any bread on him by not telling the truth.

After breaking down again in the bathroom stall at work, I asked my boss if I could take off the rest of the week. I told him I needed to go to my grandfather's funeral in Mississippi, and he allowed me to leave.

On my way home, I stopped to pick up some groceries at Schnucks on West Florissant Avenue. Whenever I'm stressed, I always pig out. My cart was full of junk: potato chips, cookies, ice cream, and pizza rolls. You name it, it was there. I stood in the long line and picked up a magazine to keep myself occupied.

"Shorty?" I heard a voice from behind. It was Stephon.

"Hey, Stephon," I said, giving him a hug. "How are you?"

"Naw, the question is how you are? I hope you're feeling better since your visit the other day. You had me kind of worried."

"Worried for what? I know you didn't think I would kill myself or anything like that, did you?"

Stephon chuckled. "Nah, nothing like that. I was just worried. You've been with my cousin for a long time and you kind of like family."

"Yeah, well, even family can snake you sometimes." I reached in my cart and laid my groceries on the conveyor belt.

Stephon reached in and helped me—until he came across a bag of maxi pads. He dropped them back in the cart like they were on fire or something.

"Now, if you're going to help, those need to be put up there too," I said, smiling. He laughed.

"I'll let you handle those."

As the cashier rang up my groceries and provided me with a total, I looked at her like she was crazy. I didn't think I'd put that many things into my cart. I reached into my purse to pay her.

"I got it." Stephon gave the cashier his credit card.

"Stephon, thanks, but I think I can handle my grocery bill."

"No problem. Besides, I owe you one anyway."

"For what?"

Stephon didn't say anything. He put my bags into the cart and pushed it out the door. When we got to my car, he loaded everything into my trunk.

"There you go, Shorty. Don't say I ain't never done nothing for you."

"I never did, but why do you owe me one? That's what I want to know."

"Because I really felt bad about the lie I told you the other day. I love my cuz and everything, but I seriously think y'all need to work it out. When I talked to him Sunday, he sounded pretty down. Why don't you call him?"

"Stephon, please stay out of this. You of all people know Jaylin has done nothing but manipulate me over the years. Why would you even want me to continue to be with him?"

"Because you're miserable; he's miserable. Don't make sense for two people who love each other to be miserable."

"You know better than I do Jaylin isn't miserable. He's got that . . . that thing over there with him and he's enjoying every minute of the day being with her. You didn't see the way he was all into her; I did. Just standing here thinking about it hurts so badly—" I got teary-eyed again.

"Nokea, I didn't mean to upset you. But you know how Jaylin is. After he gets what he wants from her, he'll be knocking at your door."

"Well, he can knock all he wants to. I will no longer be there for him."

Stephon tried to persuade me to give Jaylin another chance, but I got in my car and waved good-bye. I hated conversing with Stephon about Jaylin; all he was going to do was go back and tell him.

When I got home, I put away my groceries and slipped into my nightgown. I lay in bed and watched Mandy Murphey on Fox 2 News while eating chocolates. This was the life. I wished I could lay there and eat chocolates forever.

After a while, the news depressed me with black folks killing each other, so I turned off the TV and grabbed a book to read. I quickly got bored with that and picked up the phone next to me. My conversation with Stephon made me want to speak to Jaylin, so I dialed his number. But when I got to the sixth digit, I hung up. He was the one who wronged me, so why should I pick up the phone to call him? Besides, I knew he probably wasn't home from work yet. The thought of leaving him a message crossed my mind. I could say I forgot something or I needed him to pick up something he'd left at my place. I struggled with the idea for a moment then I dropped the thought.

I turned the radio on Foxy 95.5 and listened to my girl Niecy Davis. The music helped relax me, and before I knew it, I had dozed off.

I was awakened by a knock at the door. My house was pitch black, so I knew it had to be pretty late. I glanced out the peephole to see who it was. It was Jaylin, standing on my porch with his hands in his pockets and his head down. I backed away from the door because the look of him always made my heart melt. I didn't want my hormones answering the door for me. When I didn't answer, he banged harder.

"Nokea, I know you're in there. I saw the light come on. Open the door, baby."

Wasn't any sense in me trying to pretend I wasn't home, so I cracked the door enough to tell him I didn't want to talk.

"What do you mean you don't want to talk? You've always been able to talk to me. Open the door."

"This time is different, Jaylin. I don't want to talk. That's why I got my number changed. Please, just go away."

"No, Nokea. I'm not leaving, so you might as well open the door."

I hesitated, but then admitted to myself how badly I wanted to see him. I needed him to say that he was sorry. I wanted him to know how much his actions had hurt me. I took the chain off the door and opened it.

"Now, that wasn't so hard, was it?" he said. He walked in and took off his cap and jacket. He obviously intended to stay a while.

"Why are you here?" I said softly. "Let's just move on, okay?"

"Are you crazy? Move on my ass. You know damn well we were meant to be together, so why you tripping?" He moved closer to me, but I pushed him back.

"Would you please just go? I don't need this right now."

"I told you once, I'm not leaving until you forgive me. Just a couple of weeks ago you made me a promise. You said that when things got rough between us, you wouldn't leave. As long as I've known you, you've always been a woman of your word. What's the sudden change?"

I raised my voice and pointed my finger at him. "I handled you being with other women for nine years, but I can't do it anymore. Especially after I saw you making love to Scorpio in the shower. That just did something to me, Jaylin, and no matter how hard I try to erase that day from my memory, I can't. The thought of it sticks with me twenty-four/seven, and—"

Jaylin saw me getting emotional and stepped up to put his arms around me. He rubbed my back and kissed my forehead. I wanted to push him away, but his touch was what I needed.

"Baby, I don't know what to say. I was wrong. If that's what you need to hear me say, then yes, I was wrong. But please don't hold it against me for the rest of our lives. Without you, life has been very lonely for me."

The pressure was on. I couldn't even respond to him. Jaylin had me in the palms of his hands and my emotions were all over the place. He lifted my chin to kiss me, and I felt myself getting weaker by the minute.

"Let me make love to you," he whispered in my ear. "I want to hold you tonight, and if you still feel the same way tomorrow, then I promise I will never come here again."

I stood in silence, and he took my hand and led me to my bedroom. He removed my nightgown, and even though I knew better than to give myself to him, I couldn't ignore how much I wanted to feel him again. I couldn't deny how much I still loved him, and now was another opportunity to show him just that.

He rubbed his hands over my naked body and felt my moist insides. The thought of him making love to Scorpio was still fresh in my mind, but when he opened my legs and did what he knew best, I squirmed like a slithering snake.

I gave him a good taste of me, and then he inserted himself. Tears rolled down my face in the dark, but I was willing to bear the pain this time. I wanted this man so much it was almost frightening. Yes, I was vulnerable, and I wasn't sure if Jaylin had taken advantage of that. It was too late for me to think about his motives. I had made a promise to myself to never let this happen again, but there I was enjoying every deep stroke he gave me. His loving was so satisfying to me, and after a while, the pain seemed to ease up a bit. I allowed him to proceed without any interruptions.

Jaylin got tense, and when I felt the muscles in his butt tighten, I squeezed it. We both took several deep breaths, and as they slowed, he rolled on his back. The shameful guilt I had for allowing this to happen immediately kicked in. I felt like such a fool for the choice I'd made. Jaylin almost looked like he was smirking. Why in the heck was I continuing to make things easy for him?

I turned to my side. "Jaylin, if you don't mind, I'd like to be alone."

He turned face-to-face with me and rubbed my hip. "Come on baby. I thought you wanted me to stay the night."

"No. I really need to be alone right now. What we shared was nice, but I need time to get my head straight."

Jaylin sat up and shook his head. "I'm not going to pressure you, Nokea. I told you, if you're not feeling this relationship anymore then let me know."

"Oh, I am definitely feeling us, but I can't be with you under these conditions. There's just no way I can do it."

"Hey, whatever you say. I hope you find a place in your heart to forgive me. That way, we can get on with our relationship."

"Is this what we're calling relationships these days? You screw whoever you want to and I'm there for you no matter what? That doesn't seem quite fair to me." I turned and pulled the cover over me. Jaylin bent down and gave me a tiny peck on the tip of my nose.

"It is what it is, Nokea. The ball is in your court,

and it's up to you to shoot it. Get some rest. I hope to hear from you tomorrow," he said before leaving.

I realized how tough it was going to be for me to distance myself from him. All I had to do was not open the door, but when I saw him, I got weak. There had to be somewhere I could go for help. I was losing respect for myself, slowly but surely. But, my word as my bond, I promised to never open up my legs to him again, unless he made a commitment to me.

15

JAYLIN

"Didn't I tell you I'm the man?" I yelled while talking to Stephon at work with my feet propped up on the desk.

"Man, I just can't believe she gave in like that. When I saw her at the grocery store, she seemed so confident it was over."

"Yeah, she was confident all right. Confident that she wanted some of this good loving I be dishing out."

"Jay, you know you crazy. That woman just loves your black ass, that's all. If she could get past that, she'd be okay. As for Felicia—damn, she just trying to get laid."

"And so am I. That's why when she came here yesterday, I waxed that ass all on my desk and had her begging for more."

"You wild dog. Straight up fucking wild. How much pussy can a nigga get? After one time a day my ass be wore out! If I had to go two or three times, that would kill me. And then with different women . . . shit, I hope you're strapped up good."

"Well, you know how it is. Sometimes I do, sometimes I don't. Depending on who it is. With Felicia I most definitely break one out because ain't no telling who been up in that. But Nokea, that's all good. I'm the only brotha who will ever have a mark on her stuff. As for Scorpio, it depends. Her shit be so good, I just like to get the real deal. You know what I mean?"

"Yeah, sure in the hell do. Been there and done that, so I ain't knocking you at all, my brotha. Hey, listen, while I have you on the phone, Ray-Ray proposed to that skinny dark chick he's been dating for six months. They haven't set a date yet, but he told me to tell you to hook a brotha up with some nice females at his bachelor party. He's looking for something a little extravagant—none of that strip club action, please. We've been there, done that."

"I agree, and tell the brotha I said congrats. I'll see what I can do." Angela walked in and told me one of my clients was there to see me. "Say, man, I'll call you later." Stephon hung up and Angela let Higgins into my office.

"Jaylin, what's up, bro?" he said, shaking my hand.

"Hey, how you doing, Mr. Higgins? Have a seat, sir." He sat down and lit up a Cuban cigar. The smell of it drove me crazy, but since he was one of my major clients, what the hell?

"Jaylin, I never received confirmation on those additional shares I talked to you about. I checked the market today and this company is moving. How are we looking?"

Damn. I'd forgotten to take care of those shares for Higgins. Focusing so much time on Scorpio's good loving and rekindling my relationship with Nokea, it totally slipped my mind.

"Let me see . . ." I said, turning around to my monitor. I hit the keyboard and took a quick glance at my own stocks. "Looks like everything is moving right along. You were right about this company. It's moving at a fast pace."

"That's good to know."

I checked Higgins' mutual funds and gave him an accurate number as to how much they'd gone up. I also shared with him how much money he'd made in the past week. He was pleased.

"Any extra money I make, Jaylin, is good news. What I would like for you to do is call up some of my friends who are clients of yours and let them know what it would cost to buy into Mason Technologies immediately. That way, hopefully, we'll all be rich like you." He laughed and looked for an ashtray to dump his ashes.

"Here you go." I handed him a coaster. "I don't have ashtrays in here because the smell of smoke sometimes irritates me. And I'll be happy to call everyone to let them know about Mason Technologies."

"Thanks, Jaylin. I'm not going to take up much more of your time. Just keep in touch; you've been a hard man to catch up with lately. I guess that lady who was screwing your brains out the other day is keeping you busy, huh?"

"Nah, nothing like that. Anyway, sorry for the interruption. She just couldn't get enough of me that day," I said, laughing. He laughed too, reached into his pocket and gave me an envelope.

"Here's a little something extra my wife and I put together for all your hard work and dedication to making us very wealthy people. I trust you with my life and hope you'll continue to make good decisions so we can have everything we've always dreamed of."

"Thanks, Mr. Higgins." I reached for the envelope. "And as always, you can count on me."

I could hear Higgins outside my office as he flirted with Angela. If I didn't know any better, I'd think they had slept together before. Angela was a gold digger and looked for anybody who had money. She tried to work that thang on me, but I wasn't having it. As soon as she married my boss' son, I ended it. He treated her like a queen, but for her, that still wasn't enough. He even told her she didn't have to work, but she insisted on being out of the house. That's what I have a beef with some men about; always wanting their women to stay at home and shit. Two salaries are always better than one. I don't care what anybody says.

Shortly after I heard Higgins leave, I opened the envelope he'd given me. Enclosed was a check for $25,000 and two tickets for a cruise to the Bahamas. Seven days and six nights. Already paid for. I'd been to the Bahamas before with Felicia, but we argued so much it was ridiculous. So, taking her again was definitely out of the question. Nokea hadn't called all day, so it was obvious she needed more time to get herself together. I'd take Scorpio. She would be perfect to kick it with in the Bahamas. Besides, with her I knew I'd be getting my fuck on every single day.

Before I called her, I called Higgins and left him a thank you message addressed to him and his wife. I then sat back and tried to fix the problem I had with not buying his shares when he asked me to. The only solution was for me to make up the loss of profit with my own money. I wasn't happy about doing so, but I had no one to blame but myself.

I called Angela in my office to see if she would stay late and help me make some calls to get Higgins' buddies invested as well. They had been nothing but good to me, so the more money I made them, the better off I would be.

Angela and I were in the office until 9:00 that night trying to cut deals over the phone for Higgins' buddies. Since they made up at least sixty percent of my salary, I didn't care how long it took. Exhausted, I took off my jacket and sat back on the small hunter green sofa in my office.

Angela came in with a glass of wine for each of us; she knew how well wine relaxed me. She sat on the plush carpeted floor in front of me with her legs folded. I could see right up her short skirt, and I'm sure her intention was to let me see.

She came over to me on her knees. "Jaylin, let's give a toast."

"Toast to what? To how tired I am?"

"Well, if that's what you want to toast to, then go right ahead. But I was thinking more like a toast to mo' money, mo' money, and mo' money."

"Now, I'll drink to that." We both laughed and clinked our glasses together. She tapped my glass so hard the wine splashed on my expensive pants. I jumped so the wine wouldn't seep through them. "Damn, Angela, what are you doing?"

"Sorry. I didn't mean for that much to spill on you."

"What do you mean, you didn't mean for that much to spill on me? Did you do that shit purposely?"

She looked at me and smiled. "You know I did. I was hoping you'd take them off and send a sista home with a smile on her face like you did for Felicia the other day."

I walked over to my desk and dabbed my pants with a handkerchief.

"Angela, I ain't trying to go there with you. Old man Schmidt would kill me if he knew what we used to be doing up in here, and you know he works late every single night. Sorry, baby, but I can't take the risk anymore. Besides, ain't your husband satisfying your needs?"

"No, he's really not. I mean, he's satisfying my financial needs, but I'm always up to having sex with you."

"Um . . . sorry to hear that your needs aren't being met. I can't help you though. Once again, there's too much risk involved."

While I continued to dab my pants, Angela closed the door then came over and kneeled down in front of me again.

"Let me at least have these pants cleaned for you." She started to unbuckle my belt. I grabbed her hand, unable to believe I was turning down some pussy.

"Look, I can't go out like that, Angela. Sorry."

"All I want to do is taste it, Jaylin. You don't have a problem with me doing that, do you?"

My thang was already on the rise, and taking a risk might be worth it. At this point, there wasn't no sense in trying to reject her. A little blowjob never hurt anyone.

I closed my eyes and allowed her to go to work. She must have really been practicing on her husband because her slurps and deep throat had me on cloud nine. She wasn't good at this before, but had earned herself a B+ tonight. I was in a trance, leaned back in my chair, until I heard two people talking. Angela hopped up and I quickly buttoned my pants.

No sooner had I zipped them and sat at my desk than Schmidt knocked and stuck his head in my office. He introduced Angela to one of his friends, and I scooted my chair close to my desk so he wouldn't notice my wet pants.

"How do you do, Roy? It's nice to finally meet you," she said, nervously shaking his hand.

"Doug wasn't kidding. He does have a beautiful wife. It's good to finally meet you too."

"And this here is my top investment broker, Jaylin 'Millionaire' Rogers. Jaylin, this is Roy Johnson. He's going to be our new sales and marketing manager."

I reached out and shook Roy's hand. "Nice to meet you. Good luck on your new position."

"Thanks," he said.

"Jaylin, Angela, we'll let you two get back to work. Angela, Doug said he's been trying to reach you. Give him a call to let him know when you'll be leaving."

"I sure will, Pops. I'll call him right now." She gave him a kiss on the cheek.

Now he had the fragrance of my goods on his face. Never—and I mean never—again.

I made that clear to Angela, and she left my office with an attitude. Afterward, I closed my door and picked up the phone to call Scorpio. Angela had gotten me pretty worked up, so I figured I'd finish off the night with some workable pussy. The sound of Scorpio's sexy voice caused me to display my pearly whites.

"Say, baby, it's Jaylin."

"I know who this is. Not only that, but I know what you want."

"Oh yeah? And what might that be?"

"You want me to meet you at your place and make love to you all night long."

"You're partially correct. First, I want to invite you to go on a cruise with me to the Bahamas in a couple of weeks, and then I want you to meet me at my place tonight so we can exchange some juices."

"What if I tell you I'm busy or I can't find a sitter? Will you call someone else to exchange some juices with tonight?"

"Good question, baby, but nobody can make my juices flow the way you do. So, what time should I expect you?"

"Your juice sounds delicious. Give me an hour and I'll be there. Don't have me waiting, because I don't like to wait when I'm anxious."

"You, wait on me? Shit . . . never. I'm leaving the office now."

"And, Jaylin, I like swimming pools too. Why don't I meet you in the pool area? Let's say the Jacuzzi?"

"I'll go home and get it warm for you."

I hung up and got my ass out of the office as quickly as I could. Angela and I took the elevator down to the parking garage, and when I rushed her to her car, she started in with the questions.

"Jaylin, who were you talking to? I heard you tell somebody you were on your way," she said with one leg hanging out of her car.

"Angela, don't go questioning me. We don't have that type of relationship, so please don't start. And as for what happened in my office today, it will never happen again. If those two had been just a minute earlier, we could've lost our jobs."

"Now, you know that isn't going to happen. Pops trusts me and so does Doug. They have no idea what went on with us in the past, and they surely don't know what's up with us now."

"Well, good, because there's nothing going on with us now and I'd like to keep it that way. So, good night and be careful." I closed her door.

She rolled her big bubble eyes and started her car. I didn't care how mad she was, I just couldn't continue to do shit like that. My career meant more to me than anything.

Somehow, I managed to get stuck in traffic on Manchester Road, since I tried to take a shortcut. But by the time I got home, Scorpio's car wasn't there, so I figured I had time to warm up the Jacuzzi and put on some relaxing music. I got out of my work clothes, showered, and went into the kitchen to get some chocolate-covered strawberries I had in the refrigerator just in case I wanted to set the mood.

I went to the pool area and turned on the Jacuzzi so it would be nice and warm before Scorpio came. Then I put on some soft music and stepped my naked body into the Jacuzzi and waited for her. I poured myself a glass of wine and set her glass next to the tray of strawberries. I left the front door slightly cracked so she wouldn't have to knock when she came.

As the water bubbled and steamed, I closed my eyes

and dozed off. Shortly after, I was awakened by the touch of her soft, wet lips. But when I opened my eyes, I saw that is was Felicia standing over me.

"Are you expecting someone, Jaylin? I know you ain't sitting out here butt naked in the Jacuzzi by yourself."

"Yes, I am expecting someone, Felicia. Why don't you go home and I'll give you a call tomorrow."

"Nope, can't do that. I've been leaving you messages all day long and you haven't returned any of them. I thought we had an understanding."

"Look, I've been busy! That's why I haven't returned your phone calls. I planned on doing so, but I just hadn't gotten around to it."

"But you've gotten around to calling some other bitch over here. Who is it? I hope it ain't who I think it is."

"Felicia, it ain't none of your business. I told you before, don't be coming over here unannounced. It used to be cool, but since you tripped like you did the other day, the rules have changed."

"So, you got rules now, huh? I'm scared of you. Look, I'll let you have your little shindig over here tonight, but when I call you, you need to return my phone calls."

"And you need to go before my company gets here."

Felicia put her hand in the water and tried to grab my goods. I grabbed her hand and asked her again to leave.

As soon as Felicia stood up, Scorpio stepped into the pool area and closed the sliding glass doors behind her. She looked delicious in a red fishnet bikini that revealed everything. She dropped her flowered wrap at the door and strutted over to me like Felicia didn't exist. Her long, shiny hair was slicked back, and her curls dangled on the left side of her shoulder.

Felicia's eyes looked like they were shooting ammunition. She couldn't keep them off Scorpio's stunning beauty.

When Scorpio picked up her wineglass and sat in the Jacuzzi beside me, it was time for me to escort Felicia out. I stepped out of the water, bare-bodied and all, and told Felicia it was time to go.

"I'm leaving, Jaylin, but would you at least have the decency to walk me to the door?"

I bent down and gave Scorpio a kiss. As expected, she made it juicy and teased my lips with her tongue. "I'll be right back. Don't you go nowhere," I said.

"Hurry. I can't wait much longer," she said, starting to remove her bikini top.

Felicia rolled her eyes and shook her head. I pulled the sliding door over and motioned for Felicia to follow. When we got to the living room, she paused and poked her finger at my chest.

"This is ridiculous and you know it. This bitch ain't nothing but a freak! The both of you walking around here with no damn clothes on like it's a freak fest or something." She gazed at my stuff. I knew damn well she wished it was her in that Jacuzzi instead of Scorpio.

"Look, Felicia, get your fucking finger off my chest. This is what's going to happen when you come over here without an invitation. I'm not doing this to hurt you, but when you go searching for shit, you're definitely going to find it. So stop searching. I'll call you tomorrow. Just maybe, I'll see you on Friday."

"To hell with Friday, Jaylin. One day, you're going to regret everything you're doing to me."

"You're doing it to yourself, Felicia. You for damn sure can't blame me for nothing."

She slammed the door and Mama's picture fell off the mantle. I walked over and picked it up. I stood for a moment and thought about Mama. I wondered if she was proud of me. Wondered if she knew what I'd been through after she died. And I wondered if she was upset with me for not being with Nokea.

I placed my lips on her picture and put it back on the mantle.

When I went back outside, Scorpio was still in the Jacuzzi, enjoying the chocolate-covered strawberries. I got back in, and after she straddled my lap, I wrapped my arms around her. She put a strawberry in my mouth then poured wine on her breasts for me to suck them. Her nipples were at full attention when she intervened during my performance.

"Jaylin?"

"Yeah, baby."

"I don't ever want to see Felicia over here again. She's becoming a pain, and I don't like to be hurt."

"I'll take care of her. Don't you worry your pretty little self about Felicia because she won't be coming back any time soon."

I put Scorpio into position and prepared myself for a long and enjoyable night. As for Felicia, she had to go. Not only because Scorpio wanted me to let her go, but because she was becoming a pain in the ass. I didn't know how I would break it to her, but I knew ending it with her had to be done soon.

16

FELICIA

Friday came before I knew it, and Jaylin was a no show. I didn't know how to handle his rejection. It sure as hell didn't feel good. This Scorpio bitch took up too much of his time, even time away from Nokea, I suspected. I had no clue when he saw her. It appeared that she was put on the back burner like I was. If that was true, then maybe it was time for us to pull together and try to get Jaylin to come back to reality. He was somewhere in la-la land thinking that all he needed to satisfy him was Scorpio.

She was nasty-looking to me. I didn't care what he said. I mean, she had a nice body, but did she have to flaunt that motherfucker in front of females? I wasn't interested in looking at the ho, but any time a woman got a red rose tattooed on the back of her ass, you can't help but notice. She might as well have shown up naked. Tiny-ass red bikini wasn't hiding an inch.

Jaylin didn't think I noticed, but he was full of lust as he watched her. I was afraid he'd fuck her right there in front of me. He never looked at me like that, and I can't even recall if I'd seen him look at Nokea like that. He'd definitely fallen for this hoochie, and the only one who could come between them was Nokea.

When I got home from work, I called Nokea's house. Her number had been changed, and when I tried her cell phone, I found out that had been changed too. What was up? Something wasn't right, and I was anxious to find out what it was.

I called my ex-boyfriend, Damion, and told him to meet me at my house later on tonight. I refused to be alone on another Friday night, and since Jaylin was full of games, Damion would just have to do.

I changed clothes and decided to pay Miss Homebody a visit at her house off New Halls Ferry Road. I knew she would be stupid enough to let me in, especially if I pretended I was looking out for what was in Jaylin's best interests.

Her black Acura Legend was parked in front of her house. I could see a light on in her bedroom and that was it. The rest of the house was dark. I rang the doorbell repeatedly, not caring if she was asleep or not. I could see her through the glass door.

"Who is it?" she asked, as if she really couldn't tell it was me.

"Nokea, it's me, Felicia. I just want to talk to you for a minute, if you don't mind."

"About what, Felicia? You and I have nothing to talk about."

"Yes we do, so please open the door. This is about Jaylin and his new woman. He and I got into a confrontation, and I wondered if you could help me with something. Please."

I couldn't believe I begged her to talk, but I was desperate. She opened the door looking terrible. I'd never seen her look so bad. The bags underneath her eyes showed stress. She looked as if she hadn't slept in days; her hair was in tiny pink rollers, and her pink bathrobe was a wrinkled mess.

"Come in, but make it quick. I'm tired and need to get some rest." She put her hands in her pockets and stood by the door.

"Do you mind if I at least have a seat? It won't take long, but I really need to talk to you about something."

We walked over to her sofa in the living room. She had really jazzed up the place since I'd last seen it. I'd come to her house three months after I met Jaylin and confronted her. He told me about their relationship, but I wanted to find out just how serious it was. I followed him to her place, and after he left, I went to door. At the time, Nokea seemed confident that Jaylin would dump me right away. She said it was something he routinely did, but I assured her that I wasn't going anywhere anytime soon. Four years later, I was still here.

From what I could see, her place wasn't that spectacular then, but now she had it fixed up like an African exhibit. All kinds of black art covered the walls, and she had a black statue in one corner that damn near reached the twelve-foot ceiling in her living room. She had a plush loveseat and sofa covered in Nefertiti cloth, and an old black baby grand piano jazzed up the room. A huge honey-mustard, green, and burgundy rug with swirls covered the shiny hardwood floors, and the burning candles gave the room a nice subtle fragrance.

"So, Felicia, what trouble are you here to cause today?"

"I'm not here to cause any trouble. I just want to find out where things stand with you and Jaylin. I know he's been spending a lot of time with Scorpio and I wondered if you've seen him lately."

"What do you mean, he's been spending a lot of time with Scorpio? How do you know how much time he spends with her?"

"I know because every time I call him she's over there. The other night, I stopped by his place and they were in his Jacuzzi having sex," I said, spicing things up like I had seen it for myself.

"So, you had the pleasure of seeing them in action too, huh? I walked in on them in the shower, and after that, I ended it. Well, I tried to end it."

"What? You saw them together in his shower? What did he say?"

"He didn't say much. You know the usual excuses he makes for his behavior. He came over Monday night and apologized. And, stupid me, I was so vulnerable that I forgave him."

"Monday night, huh? I had just seen him Monday afternoon. I went to his office and he couldn't keep his hands off me. Tried to have sex with me right then and there. I went ahead and gave in, but I told him if he wanted to make love to me again, it would have to be in a better place."

Nokea was quiet. She turned her head, and I could see her throat move in and out as she took a hard swallow.

"Felicia, after work, Jaylin came over here Monday

night and made love to me. I felt something wasn't right, but I let him do it anyway. How could I be so stupid?" She yelled and tightened her fist as she took a seat on the piano bench.

Her confirmation that she and Jaylin had already been intimate rubbed me the wrong way. Now I felt as if she was a bigger competition for me, and getting rid of Scorpio wasn't going to be enough. I had to get rid of her too, but I didn't want to let her know that her words had gotten underneath my skin.

"How could we both be so stupid, Nokea? I'm just as guilty, so don't feel bad. The question is what are we going to do about it? If you want things to change, then we got to figure out what we can do to change them."

"I'm not doing anything. I don't want Jaylin anymore. I haven't talked to him since Monday, and for me, that's only the first step. If you want to fight for him, you go right ahead. But you won't be battling with me."

"Nokea, you know you've said that a million times before. What makes you think this time it's a for sure thing?"

"Because I know. I feel it in my heart and in my soul. The only thing I need to do is figure out a way to get my energy back. I feel beat. I'm exhausted from all this crying, and it's wearing me down."

"I don't mean any harm, Nokea, but I can tell. I ain't never seen you look like this. The difference between you and me is Jaylin will never bring me down no matter how hard he may try."

"No, Felicia. The difference between you and me is I love him and you don't. That's why it's harder for me than it is for you. I'm not saying you don't care for him, but that's all it is. You will be able to walk away whenever you eventually get tired. Me, it's going to take time. More time than I anticipated. But for now, as long as I don't see him, I'm doing okay."

Even though I hated to admit it, Nokea was right. I didn't love Jaylin as much as she did—but if I couldn't have him, no one would.

I left Nokea's house on a good note. I didn't tell her what I intended to do, but she made it perfectly clear that she was out of it. I couldn't blame her; she had to be the one who suffered the most pain from Jaylin. I had only stepped into this mess four years ago and was already exhausted from the female bullshit.

When I got back home, I called Jaylin and left him another nasty message for dissing me again on Friday night. I changed clothes and waited for Damion to come over so I could get some type of satisfaction for the night. I was sure he'd be lacking somewhere, someway, or somehow, and that's why I had to make sure Jaylin's and my relationship got back on track. Soon.

17

NOKEA

It had been three whole weeks since I last talked to or saw Jaylin. I went to Infiniti Styles on the corner of Chambers and West Florissant Avenue to get my hair done, and then I shopped at the Galleria to find some outfits for the fall. As far as I was concerned, I was back in action. Not only did I look good again, but I felt good as well.

That was until late Sunday night. I'd eaten some greasy fried chicken at Pat's place, and it had my stomach upset. I went to the bathroom and threw up. I thought it would make me feel better, but it didn't; I felt nauseated and faint.

I went home, lay down in my bed with a cold rag across my forehead, and tried to figure out what was wrong with me. By morning, I had thrown up again. I called my doctor to make an appointment, and then called my boss and told him I would be late. The thought of food poisoning crossed my mind because for some reason, the chicken didn't taste right to me.

I arrived at Dr. Beckwith's office in the Central West End about nine-thirty in the morning. Immediately, the nurse called my name, so I didn't have to wait long. When Dr. Beckwith came in, he asked me all kinds of questions. When I told him what my symptoms were, he said it didn't sound like I had food poisoning and told me he wanted to give me a pregnancy test. Since I hadn't missed my period, I knew it wasn't possible. Besides, Jaylin and I only had sex one and a half times. Still, I knew one time is all it takes, so I anxiously waited for the results.

Dr. Beckwith came back into the room and pulled a chair next to me. He had a smile on his face as he slid his pen along the side of his ear.

"Nokea, I have good news and more good news. Which one would you like to hear first?" I'd been with Dr. Beckwith since I was a little girl, and he always joked around with me when something was wrong.

"Well, Dr. Beckwith, if it's double good news, then let's hear it."

"First, you don't have food poisoning, and second, you're going to have a baby."

The grin on my face vanished.

"Wha . . . what did you say?"

"Yes, Nokea, you're pregnant. And we're going to do everything possible to make sure you have a healthy baby."

I was speechless. When Dr. Beckwith left the room, I dropped my head and burst into tears. I never thought I would have a baby out of wedlock. Mama and Daddy wouldn't be happy about the news. I knew they'd be disappointed in me and Jaylin.

For the last few months, I had really been a disappointment to myself. Why did I have to make so many messed-up decisions? Decisions that cost me big-time.

Dr. Beckwith's nurse came in and congratulated me. She gave me a hug and immediately noticed that I'd been crying.

"Are those tears of joy?" she asked, helping me off the examination table.

"No . . . I don't know. I'm confused right now. Really, I don't know how I feel."

"I know it comes as a shock today, but once you get home and think about how much happiness this baby is going to bring to your life, you'll feel a whole lot better. It's normal for you to feel the way you are. Just don't go making any decisions until you've had time to think about it."

"Thank you," I said, giving her another hug.

I called my boss and asked for some personal time off. Hearing how anxious I sounded, he didn't seem to have a problem with it.

I drove down Euclid Avenue and thought about how Jaylin would feel about this. I knew how much he loved his daughter, who disappeared with her mother years ago, so I was positive he wouldn't have a problem loving the baby I carried. Would this baby finally change our lives? Was this a sign from God we needed to be together as a family? The big question was, when would I break the news to him—or would I do it at all?

I needed advice, so I went to Barnes Jewish Hospital on Kingshighway, where Pat worked, to see if she would take an early lunch with me. She told her boss it was urgent, grabbed her purse, and we headed to the Pasta House.

"So, why are you dragging my butt out of the office like this couldn't wait until I got home?" Pat asked. The waiter poured our water and handed us menus. I wanted to wait until he was gone to answer Pat's question.

"If you don't mind," I said, "give us about ten minutes and we'll be ready to order." The waiter nodded and walked away.

"Okay, Nokea, out with it. He's gone, so what's on your mind?"

I reached my hands across the table and held hers. "Pat, I'm having a baby. The doctor confirmed it this morning, and I'm confused about what I need to do."

She squeezed my hands tighter and yelled. "Girl, I'm so happy for you!" Her voice lowered. "But please don't tell me it's Jaylin's baby. I know he's the only one you've been with, but just make up somebody, please."

I laughed with her.

"Girl, you know I can't lie like that. You know its Jaylin's. The question is, what am I going to do? I haven't called him in weeks, and I've been working hard trying to get him out of my system. And just when I thought things were going well, bam—I'm pregnant."

"I know I'm your best friend, but when it comes to Jaylin, I'm not one to give you advice."

"Yes, you are, Pat. You've always given me good advice. I just never do what you tell me."

"Well, I'm going to tell you how I see it. If you decide to listen to me, then fine. If you don't, I won't be mad."

'Okay, that's fair enough. I just need to hear your input. Then you can tell me how disappointed you think my very religious parents will be."

"I don't think your parents will be disappointed at all, especially since they like Jaylin."

"You mean as much as they used to like Jaylin. I told Mama about what happened and she told me to move on with my life. Daddy came by to see me the other day, and when I cried on his shoulder about our ups and downs, he wasn't too happy. Actually, he said he was going by Jaylin's place to have a few words with him about how he's been treating me lately. Of course, I stopped him."

"Your parents love you. They'll understand. You're a grown woman, and I don't think they're going to be disappointed in their thirty-year-old daughter for having a baby out of wedlock. You have a good job, and you'll definitely be able to provide for this baby. As for you and Jaylin, don't tell him."

"Why not?"

"I mean don't tell him right now. Wait a while. And if he starts showing you some love without knowing you're pregnant, then work things out with him. If he doesn't call or come around, then raise this baby by yourself and do the best you can. The worst thing you can do is let him think you had this baby just to trap him. If he thinks that, you're going to hear about it for the rest of your life."

"But, Pat, you know I didn't get pregnant on purpose. When he finds out, Jaylin is going to be excited."

"I'm not saying he wouldn't be. But you know how some men are. Always thinking somebody's trying to trap their ass when they're right there making that baby with you."